RESET TO ONE

Paranormal Talent Agency

Episode Two

HEATHER SILVIO

Panther Books

Published in the United States by Panther Books, Las Vegas.

Correspondence to the author may be sent to:
heather@heathersilvio.com

Cover design by Sonia Freitas at Chloe Belle Arts
https://www.ChloeBelleArts.com

ISBN (Print) 978-1-7326938-0-7
ISBN (E-book) 978-1-7326938-3-8

BOOKS BY HEATHER SILVIO

PARANORMAL TALENT AGENCY

Lights, Camera, Action (Episode One)

Reset to One (Episode Two)

That's a Wrap (Episode Three)

An Unexpected Sequel (Episode Four)

Jumping the Shark (Episode Five)

The Season Finale (Episode Six)

NON-SERIES FICTION

Not Quite Famous: A Romantic Comedy of an Actress
on the Edge

Beyond the Abyss: Tales of the Supernatural

Courting Death

NONFICTION

Special Snowflake Syndrome: The Unrecognized
Personality Disorder Destroying the World

Happiness by the Numbers: 9 Steps to Authentic
Happiness

Stress Disorders: A Healing Path for PTSD

ACKNOWLEDGMENTS

Thank you to everyone who supported this series from its original inception to completion. Special thank you to my brand new beta readers!

CHAPTER ONE

Today was my 29th birthday. Again. That's the joke, right? At some point in the latter 20th century, women decided to stay 29. So, they celebrated turning 29 every year, and their friends laughed and everyone had a good time. Forever 29. Except that I really would be forever 29. After all, I was a vampire.

And where was I on my 92nd 29th birthday? At an acting workshop organized by my new agent, Catherine Rodham, of the Peterson Talent Agency, or as individuals of my persuasion had been calling it, the Paranormal Talent Agency. Aren't we clever? In all seriousness, though, she's pretty cool – open to the other-than-human set, dating a half-incubus, and earlier this year, even helping to catch a serial killer!

On this beautiful summer evening in Las Vegas, six of us sat on uncomfortable metal folding chairs in a circle, staring at each other. Sizing each other up. Checking our internal files to see if we'd met before at an audition or on set. Catherine had done a great job mixing the group: three men and three women, race and ethnicity across the spectrum, ages from twenty-something to fifty-something, and several different species. They said don't judge a book by its cover, but after over one hundred years on the planet, I had pretty good "species" radar. Three humans, pixie, werewolf, and me. As my gaze followed the circle, I caught my breath when it landed on one of the humans. Well, now, who did we have here?

I watched his luscious full lips while he said his name. "Hi, everybody. I'm Ryan Walter." I drank in his lithe frame in the seat, glimpsed muscles at the edges of his running shorts and marathon-finisher t-shirt. An athlete. Yum.

"I recently relocated here from Los Angeles. Smaller market, I know, but I can't afford food and rent in LA." Everyone around the circle chuckled in agreement and his smile revealed perfect white teeth. I noticed, however, the smile seemed forced.

"I also work as a paralegal. It's fun and pays the bills." For an actor, he didn't hide his distress very well. But, it wasn't my concern. The auburn glint in his hair mesmerized me. Was that dyed or natural?

"I'm happy to be here." I doubted this, but nobody challenged the comment. He finished and the next person in the circle began speaking. I was definitely not listening. I noticed that Ryan's hazel green eyes, with just a fleck of gold, seemed anxious.

Our eyes met (now didn't that sound cliched) and he checked me out the way I had checked him out. I tried to see myself through his eyes. I was turned in the 1920s but gave up my preferred style for years. One of the benefits of Vegas, however, was that, much like New York City, anything went, so my eccentric style was nothing more than that. Eccentric. Short, 1920s curly blond bob over blue eyes, very pale skin, and dark red lipstick. I looked like someone called for a stereotypical 1920s flapper from Central Casting, in all honesty. At least I wore jeans with my Gatsby-inspired green tank shirt and black ankle boots. I smiled widely at Ryan, who responded by looking at the ground. Hmm, that didn't usually happen.

I realized it was time for my introduction.

"Hi, I'm Evelyn Jones. Everyone calls me Evie." Jones, of course, was my latest fake name. "I moved to Vegas from New York to get away from the cold." Everybody chuckled and nobody caught that I didn't include a time frame.

"I've been acting in independent projects for years." Decades really, but who was counting? "I'm looking forward to working with all of you." Despite my flippant attitude generally, I really was looking forward to working with them. I loved acting.

With introductions completed, the instructor, Anthony Gullo, explained the workshop plan. Without intending to, my gaze returned to Ryan, who kept checking his watch. I frowned. If he had somewhere else to be, why didn't he just go?

Anthony asked Ryan a question. His head snapped up and he looked confused. "I'm sorry, I missed that."

"Is everything okay? I notice you keep checking your watch." Kudos to Anthony for calling Ryan out.

Ryan reddened in embarrassment. "I'm sorry. I'm distracted. Personal issue."

"Anything we can do to help?" the pixie asked and her offer seemed genuine. I looked around at the others, who were nodding.

Although it seemed to me that his statement suggested he didn't want to talk about whatever was bothering him, he opened up after that single question. I felt for the guy, I really did, but honestly, was this the time and place for his therapy?

Ryan spoke haltingly. "My best friend, Jim, was arrested. For murder." Several small gasps were heard. "I know he didn't do it and I don't know what to do." His gaze moved around the circle, as though looking for an answer. Silence greeted him. Until he reached me.

I shrugged. "Not to be mean, but how do you know he didn't do it?"

"Excuse me?"

"How do you know he didn't do it?" I repeated.

He frowned. "Of course, he didn't do it."

"I understand you believe that," I tried again. "But how do you know that?"

Anthony jumped in. I suspected he regretted opening this can of worms. "Maybe we'll shelve this conversation until the break? Ryan, if you need to leave to help your friend, we'd understand."

Ryan shook his head. "I'd rather stay. There's nothing I can do until he's released on bail. Which should be sometime tonight." He checked his watch again. "I could use the distraction. Thanks."

We resumed the workshop, which went well. We all had new scenes that we worked. As we were wrapping up, I noticed in my peripheral vision Ryan was approaching. Uh-oh. I hoped I didn't upset him earlier. I sometimes had that effect on people, even when I wasn't trying.

"Evie, right?"

"Yep. Ryan?" Like we didn't both know each other's names. Such a convoluted dance humans did.

"Yes." He hesitated. "I wanted to ask you what you meant by your comments earlier."

"I didn't mean anything by them." I could see the pain on his face and I didn't want to add to it. "I was just playing devil's advocate."

"Devil's advocate? This is my friend's life." He lowered his voice. "Sorry."

"No need to apologize. I can imagine how hard this is." Certainly, in my 100+ years, I've had friends jailed. Of course, they were guilty.

"Thank you." He stopped but didn't leave. He shifted from foot to foot.

"Was there something else?"

Our eyes met again, and damned if I didn't feel something. If only he wasn't so caught up in his friend's drama. He could be fun. Oh well. His phone beeped.

"It's Jim." The color drained from his face. His reaction perplexed me. He believed Jim was innocent. Wouldn't he be happy Jim got bailed out? Although, it equally baffled me that he couldn't entertain the possibility his friend was a killer. This fascinated me.

"I need to order a Lyft," he muttered to himself and turned away, fiddling with his phone.

"Do you need a ride to pick him up?" Both of us looked shocked by my offer.

"I do. Are you sure?"

"Definitely. Let me make up for what I said." That wasn't really why I offered, I realized. I wanted to know more. I wanted to understand how he could be so sure of someone else's behavior.

His dazzling smile returned. "Thank you. I appreciate it." We exited the building together.

"Hmm," I started, as we stood next to my dark green Fiat convertible. "How tall is your friend?"

Ryan laughed, a deep unexpected rumbling that caused me to laugh in response. "He's average, I suppose. He'll fit fine."

We drove in companionable silence to the detention center to retrieve Jim. The red brick building looked like a prison and I shuddered when we entered the parking lot.

"Do you know where we need to go to get him?"

"He said he'd be waiting out front."

Big brown letters across a tan semi-circle announced we had reached our destination. Sure enough, a guy stood in front, off to the side, scuffing the toe of his shoe on the ground. He looked like a stereotypical surfer, with his bleached blond hair and lean, wiry appearance. I couldn't see his eyes from the car. My guess was blue.

"That's Jim," Ryan confirmed my unspoken assumption and I directed the car to the curb. I watched out the window while Ryan embraced his friend. They talked for a second before Jim followed Ryan to the car.

I twisted in my seat to say hello to Jim, now ensconced in the back seat, chuckling internally because I was right. His eyes were blue. Then I felt bad for my internal chuckle. Poor man. His eyes had that lost look. His face somehow already seemed wan, like he'd been in jail for months, not just long enough to be bailed out. He managed a slight smile.

"Nice to meet you, Evie. Thanks for the ride."

"No problem. Where to now?"

Silence greeted my question. I'd have thought Jim wanted to go home, given the late hour, but since nobody said anything, I went with my gut. "You guys up for a late-night snack?"

Jim looked so grateful for the suggestion that I actually felt guilty for a nanosecond, given my ulterior motive. For some reason, it bothered me that Jim was hoodwinking his friend. I was determined to show Ryan he was wrong and that I was right. People couldn't be trusted. It didn't matter how close they were to us.

Ryan suggested a Denny's midway between here and Jim's home in Southern Highlands and I started in that direction.

"How are you doing?" Ryan tried for nonchalance, like we hadn't just picked Jim up at the jail.

The silence stretched for a few blocks and I wondered if Jim was going to answer. And then he did.

"I'm not sure," he admitted. "I feel like I'm underwater. Ever since I was arrested. My lawyer hadn't been certain I'd get bail. Even without a criminal record. Because I was arrested for a felony." Jim fell silent.

Nobody said anything the rest of the way to the diner. I had so many questions, my mouth wanted to blurt them out. I refrained, figuring that maybe food would loosen Jim's tongue. After all, how could I find the holes in his story if I didn't know his story?

CHAPTER TWO

Ryan and Jim must have been trying to communicate telepathically, based on the meaningful glances they kept sharing. I, on the other hand, not possessing such skills, was bored. We'd been sitting in the diner booth for pushing fifteen minutes with no chatter. Nada. Zip. The cheerful waitress brought us waters and took our orders, egg biscuits and French fries for the guys, and nothing for me. They didn't know I couldn't eat regular food, so I said I wasn't hungry.

"I…"

Yes! Jim was starting to speak.

"I didn't kill Monica." He looked exhausted, like uttering that phrase sapped all of his strength.

"Of course, you didn't," Ryan immediately agreed. I naturally had no idea who Monica was, but Ryan seemed to.

"My wife." Jim directed this at me, as if he read my mind, though likely I had a quizzical look on my face.

"I don't know what happened," he admitted, dropping his gaze to his lap, hands locked in nervous fidgeting.

"What do you know?" I asked the question gently. I felt bad for him; he seemed genuinely saddened and scared. Still, I was on a mission.

"What happened?" Ryan added this question. Silence followed. Jim appeared to be considering what to say in response.

The waitress returned with their food, sparing Jim from having to respond. She placed the dishes, told the men to enjoy, and departed. Jim sighed deeply.

"We had gone to the theater, the one in Chinatown," he explained. "It was a longer show, so it was already after 10 when we left. Nothing seemed wrong when we got home. No lights were on in the house. No strange vehicles were parked nearby. I pulled into the garage and closed the door. All like I normally did. We entered the house from the garage and that's when we noticed something off."

"Off? What do you mean?"

"As weird as this is, Ryan, there was a smell."

"A smell?"

"Yeah. It smelled woody."

"Like the woods?"

"Not exactly. Just woody," he said, face pinched. He closed his eyes briefly. "I joked with Monica about her sneaking a guy into the house and she laughed. We assumed." He stopped. "I don't know what we assumed, to be honest. It simply never occurred to us that someone could be in the house. Like I said, no lights were on, no cars were outside, we didn't hear any sounds." I wondered if Jim was trying to convince himself almost as much as he was trying to convince us.

"We were laughing, joking about the show. I locked the door behind us and we went to the kitchen, turning lights on and off while we made our way there. Monica tossed her purse onto the counter and I grabbed a bottle of red wine to pour a couple of glasses." His recitation had the familiar feel of a story oft repeated; how many times had he already told it to the police?

Jim stopped again, the silence stretching so long that I was unsure if he would start again without a prompt. His eyes closed. Ryan and I exchanged glances. We remained quiet. Jim ate a French fry, took a sip of water. He was clearly delaying.

"You know what our kitchen looks like?" This was directed at Ryan, who nodded. "I was at the counter near the side window, pouring the glasses, when Monica screamed. I dropped the glass, it shattered. As I was turning around, I sensed movement by my head, I was overwhelmed by that woody smell. And then nothing."

He sipped more water, the glass shaking in his hand.

I tried to pay attention to Jim's physical changes, looking for the tell to suggest which parts he was lying about…or maybe just omitting. Except I found myself distracted by Ryan. His beautiful hazel eyes, so expressive, clouded over. I saw the pain in them, not only for his friend, but for his friend's wife, the murder victim.

"Nothing?" Ryan asked this quietly.

"Based on when we got home, I was unconscious for an hour. I woke up with a throbbing headache, a huge lump on the side of my head, and my wife," he stopped short. His voice hitched and tears filled his eyes. "My wife was dead beside me. Every time I close my eyes, I see her lifeless ones. And there was so much blood." Tears slid down his face, slowly at first, and then a torrent. He lowered his head to his hands, tented on the table. Was he trying to hide from us? Was it grief? Or guilt?

Ryan and I waited for him to compose himself. Jim lifted his head, eyes reddened. "I checked for a pulse and breathing, of course. It was too late. I called the police." His voice cleared, became sharp.

"I was holding her when they arrived. They arrested me for her murder. Do you want to know why?" We nodded, not daring to speak. "Because there were two bloody objects in the kitchen. That small vase on the ledge between the kitchen and the living room." This was directed at Ryan, who nodded his familiarity with the vase. "And a small frying pan. Their theory is that we got into an argument, grabbed the nearest objects, and hit each other. Because I'm stronger, I did more damage. According to my lawyer, they consider it a heat-of-the-moment killing, which is why I was charged with second degree murder."

"What about intent? What could you have been arguing about that would lead to this?" I was curious about both his answer and the police logic.

"I have no idea. My lawyer thinks they've jumped the gun. And since we weren't arguing, I don't know what they plan to say."

"Who do you think did it then?"

"I have absolutely no idea, Ryan!" Jim shouted. "The only thing out of the ordinary was the smell. And I don't know what significance that has. If any."

While Jim's distress was real enough according to his accelerated heartbeat and breathing, he had nothing. Only an alleged woody scent to suggest the presence of anybody else. It seemed as likely that Jim was the killer as it was some unknown person in the house. Not robbing it, apparently. And without a getaway car. Too many details didn't make sense in his story. My poker face must have been slipping because both Ryan and Jim were staring at me. Ryan looked angry and Jim worried.

"I know you just met me, Evie, but I swear I'm innocent," Jim insisted.

I shrugged and Ryan's eyes narrowed.

"Of course, you are, Jim. Let's get you home." Ryan threw more than enough money on the table to cover their bill, and stood. Jim and I scrambled to join him.

An uncomfortable silence filled the car while I drove Jim home. Once we arrived, he did not invite us in. He hesitated before opening the front door. We stayed in the driveway until the porch light went off. Jim had not looked back. Ryan twisted in his seat to face me.

"What is wrong with you?" He wasn't yelling but was clearly angry.

"What?" I asked innocently, though I knew what upset him.

"He lost his wife."

"He might have killed his wife."

"Are you always this thoughtless? Or heartless?"

That hurt. "Neither," I insisted. "I'm pragmatic."

"Are you kidding me?"

"No." I kept my voice steady though his irritation was starting to get to me.

"How could you tell a grieving man he killed his wife?"

"Wait a minute. I said no such thing," I argued.

"You may as well, the way you were looking at him." Ryan faced forward, staring out the front window, hands gripping his thighs, as though trying to literally get a grip on his emotions.

"I'm sorry if I upset either of you," I finally allowed. Ryan said nothing. "I have an idea."

"What?"

"If you're so certain he's innocent, prove it."

Ryan faced me again. "What are you talking about?"

"Put your money where your mouth is. Prove that Jim is innocent." Or that he was guilty, which was what I fully expected.

"You're crazy. You think he did it."

"Then prove me wrong, too."

"Why would you want to help?"

"I believe in the truth."

Ryan's body relaxed, a smile playing on his lips. I felt that unfamiliar flutter in my belly again. Maybe I had mixed motives after all.

"How would we prove Jim innocent?"

I smiled widely. "I don't know. But, they do it on TV all the time." I dropped the smile. "It's worth trying, right?"

He shook his head but the smile told me I had won him over. "Okay, let's do it. Where do we start?"

I had no idea.

CHAPTER THREE

Ryan and I mulled over possible next steps while I drove. We arrived at his one-story three-bedroom stucco home in Henderson. Cute, but looked like at least half of all the homes in Vegas. I vastly preferred my condo. I pulled into the driveway, cut the engine, and faced Ryan before he exited the vehicle.

"I really am sorry about your friend. I wasn't trying to be mean. In my experience, people always let you down, and are never what they seem." I shrugged, dropped my gaze.

Ryan sighed and I lifted my gaze back to his. "Thank you for saying so. I'm sorry that's been your experience." His unasked question of my history hung in the silence. I ignored it.

"A tale for another time." I laughed softly.

"Do you want to come in?"

His question startled me and I hesitated to respond.

"So we can continue to brainstorm," he added as if to show no illicit intentions. Heat rushed to my face at the thought of illicit intentions. My face always showed my feelings; one of the things I had hoped would be alleviated when I became a vampire. Turned out, drinking blood meant you had the same reactions you did as a human. Sigh. Oh well.

Ryan's eyes dilated and I realized I must have sighed aloud. He tentatively reached out a hand to my cheek. A thrill raced through me. His fingers gently stroked my face. I reached up, wrapped my own fingers around his, removed his touch. Now wasn't the time. He may not realize that, but I did. His expression registered surprise.

He smiled an adorably lopsided grin. "I really would like to brainstorm."

My impish smile mirrored his. "Sounds good."

We exited the convertible and he led me to his front door. Once inside, after hitting the light switch, I scanned the immediate area. Shabby chic, I thought they called the mismatched furniture and likely thrift store finds.

"It's a rental," he explained and I chuckled.

"It's cute."

"You're generous."

We both laughed and he indicated I could lead the way into the living room. I sat on the overstuffed blue corduroy couch while he headed toward the kitchen.

"This is really comfortable," I exclaimed in surprise.

"I know, right?" he agreed from the kitchen. "Do you want anything?"

"No, thank you. I'm good," I declined. I heard noises in the kitchen.

He joined me in the living room with a glass of water, sitting opposite me in a matching overstuffed chair. He wasn't smiling now.

"I don't know what to do."

"I do," I responded triumphantly. "I had an epiphany."

"Okay, spill it."

"Let's retrace Jim's steps."

Confusion showed on Ryan's face. "Retrace his steps?"

"Taking his story at face value," I paused, holding up a hand to stop Ryan from defending his friend again. "Taking his story at face value," I repeated, "nothing seemed out of the ordinary on his block, in his home, or after the attack. I agree on this point with the police. To me, it doesn't seem like a robbery gone wrong. It seems personal. And I don't mean Jim did it." Although, I kind of did. "I mean that maybe someone they encountered that day was involved. Either because they saw something or they're actually involved in the murder."

Ryan mulled this over. "Okay, that makes sense. If we retrace his steps, we should start at the theater?"

"Yes. That's the most logical place to go. My thinking is we talk to the folks at the theater who were working that night. Depending on what we get from them, we take a look at the patrons who pre-purchased tickets, since their names would be on their orders. We see if any of them have a connection to Jim or Monica."

Ryan frowned. "I don't think we'll be able to get a list of the patrons from the theater."

"You leave that to me. I may have an in for that."

Ryan and I smiled at each other, co-conspirators on the path of good. Or something like that. He looked at his watch and made a face. "It's after midnight and I have to work tomorrow."

"No worries. I'll let you go to bed." I had an involuntary flash of being in bed with Ryan that stopped me cold. Or warm, I supposed.

"What just went through your mind?"

"Why?" I answered a question with a question, delaying a response.

"I don't know. You suddenly looked like the cat that ate the canary, to use a familiar expression."

I laughed. "That's not too far off the mark," I acknowledged without explanation. He shook his head at me but smiled. I pulled out my phone. "What's your number? I'll text you mine. Go to bed. Go to work. I'll let you know when we're ready to go to the theater tomorrow night."

His phone beeped, he confirmed receipt of my text, and then we reached the front door. He paused with his hand on the knob. "Thank you. I'm not really sure why you're helping me when I know you think Jim is guilty, but I appreciate it." He opened the door.

I stared out into the Las Vegas night before meeting his eyes with a soft smile. "I believe in the truth," was still the most honest response I could give.

CHAPTER FOUR

Around the block from Ryan's home, I pulled over to the side of the road.

Are you awake?

Within seconds, Catherine sent a reply.

Yes. Need to come over?

Yep. Be there in 20.

See you soon.

One benefit of acting was that many projects shoot at night – certainly a bonus for a vampire. It was also helpful because you had a decent chance of others still being available after midnight. Of course, it further helped that this was Las Vegas.

I loved my condo building. It was in the middle of the closest thing to downtown that Vegas had off the Strip. It sat between the Arts District and Fremont Street. All the fun artsy stuff. Plus, we had gated underground parking and 24-hour security in the lobby. I parked my convertible in its underground home and headed to the twentieth floor. I bypassed my own condo and knocked on Catherine's door. Yep. We lived down the hall from each other. I had no idea when I signed with her agency, but it's been handy being neighbors. Plus, I liked her. She'd become a good friend.

The tall willowy blond opened the door, smiled sleepily at me, and held the door open for me to enter.

"You look tired. You sure you're up for company?"

"I was getting into bed," she admitted with a yawn. "Since it's after midnight, I figured it must be important. Plus, I already poured myself wine." She closed the door behind me and I followed her to the living "room". She had essentially the mirror image of my condo – decent studio with sections for a front office, dining area, living area, kitchen along the side wall, and bedroom. She even took the wall option to create a separate bedroom, on my suggestion. Floor-to-ceiling windows encircled half the space.

We faced each other on the couch.

"Okay, I'm sufficiently intrigued. What's going on?"

I summarized meeting Ryan at the workshop and volunteering to help him prove Jim's innocence.

Catherine raised her eyebrow. "This doesn't sound like you." A statement, not a question.

"I know."

"Is it because he's hot?"

Our eyes met and we busted out laughing. She knew me so well. "Believe it or not, that's not why. Though he definitely is. And it certainly doesn't hurt." I paused. "I feel like he's deluding himself. His friend probably is guilty. He just can't see it."

"How are you so sure he's guilty?"

"His story doesn't add up. An unknown, unseen assailant in a locked, dark house kills his wife and attacks him? Please. It's like a bad movie-of-the-week."

"Or *The Fugitive*."

"I doubt this is like *The Fugitive*."

"Doth the lady protest too much?"

"Not at all."

"Hey, whatever your motivation, if it helps uncover the truth, you know I fully support that."

"I know, that's why I'm here." I smiled mischievously and Catherine grinned.

"How can I help?"

"You're on the board of the Las Vegas Independent Theatre still, right?"

She nodded.

"The last place Jim and his wife went before the attack was a show there. Ryan and I plan to go tomorrow to talk to anybody who was present that night that we can. Obviously, in terms of folks in the audience, we don't think they'd just hand that info over if we asked."

"Very true," Catherine agreed. She frowned in thought.

"I can definitely get you a list of the season ticket holders who came that night. Plus, the list of advance online ticket purchases. I should also be able to get point-of-sale credit card purchases. Really, I think I can get everybody except people who paid cash. For those, your only hope is that they came with someone who's on one of the three lists of people," she concluded.

"You'd get all that for me?"

"I'll have it for you by the time you're ready to go out tomorrow night. Um, I mean, tonight," she corrected, and we both chuckled.

"Thank you so much!" I hugged her.

"Careful, don't make me spill my wine," she cautioned me.

"Never," I responded with mock solemnity.

"I'll email you the lists. You'll have them when you get up."

"Thank you again. Seriously. This is above and beyond. I really appreciate it."

Catherine looked at me in wonder. "Of course. And you're sure this has nothing to do with Ryan's hotness?"

I smiled widely and she raised an eyebrow again. "Careful," I warned her, "or your face may stick like that."

"Nice side step."

I lifted my hands in surrender. "I want to show him the truth."

"You want to show him something," she teased suggestively.

"On that note, I think I'll take my leave."

Catherine laughed and followed me to the door.

I hugged her again goodbye and she closed the door behind me. I tried, and failed, not to think of Ryan's hazel eyes and how I felt when he looked at me. I let myself into my own condo.

Locking the door behind me, I tried, and again failed, not to imagine touching his smooth skin and how warm he'd likely feel. I bypassed most of my space, decorated with colorful furniture, artwork, and knick-knacks picked up in the past hundred years.

Removing my clothing in the bedroom, I tried, and failed a third time, not to fantasize Ryan helping me with this task.

Ok, my goodness, stop. You're not a teenager. He's just a good-looking man. You've seen plenty of those in several lifetimes. I shook my head, put on utilitarian men's pajamas, and headed back out to the living space. It was still early. I had a few hours before sun up.

Along the bank of windows opposite the bedroom, my quite technologically advanced sound system (yes, that was a joke) resided against a section of concrete wall. I carefully flipped through my collection of vinyl records, looking for the right one. Ah, perfect. I placed Billie Holiday's *Lady in Satin* on the turntable, lined the needle up at the beginning, and listened to the music flow.

Before I knew it, light shone from the sun peeking over the distant mountains. Time to go to bed and recharge. The fun would begin tonight.

CHAPTER FIVE

After nearly a century as a vampire, my body sensed when the sun was setting and I was fully recharged. I woke rested and raring to go, something I had struggled with as a human. I missed dreaming, to be honest, but when you weren't really sleeping, you couldn't really dream. Though I did need to recharge. I didn't know. I couldn't really explain it. It wasn't an exact science.

The outfit I chose for tonight was another mix of 1920s and present day. Jeans for daily wear were hands down my favorite fashion invention and I wore them most days. Today, I chose a jeweled headband holding my platinum curls in the classic 20s 'do and topped the outfit with a solid turquoise peasant top.

Warmth flooded me from the red liquid I grabbed out of the fridge on my way to the office area. Yes, I drank blood. No, I didn't kill people for it. Turned out a vampire didn't need fresh blood. I mean, it tasted better, sure. But, strictly speaking, it just had to be human. After this long on the planet, plugged in to the right sources, I got it delivered. What could I say? I knew a guy.

In a few seconds, the laptop was up and I was checking email. Catherine's popped out at number one. *Here are the lists we talked about.* She attached three documents to the email. I opened each and sent them to the printer. While the machine spat the documents out, I sent a quick text to Ryan, ignoring the surge within me, an almost electrical current that I recognized as lust. Certainly not my heart fluttering, since I didn't have a heartbeat. Definitely real interest, though, and it had been a while, to say the least. This knocked me sideways for a second. I sat with the feeling, wondering at it, almost like a child. How strange. I was excited to spend time with this human – and my goal was to show him his friend was a killer. Hmm. That did not bode well, I supposed.

I refocused on my phone and texted Ryan.

Are you still free tonight for the theater?

Yep.

Bring your laptop…

Will do.

Pick you up in 20?

See you then.

A glance out the window confirmed the sun had not quite set and I grimaced. I grabbed the papers off the printer, my purse off the hook by the door, and headed downstairs to the parking garage. Once in the convertible, I headed to pick up Ryan.

The few remaining rays of the waning daylight stung when they reached me through the front windshield. Contrary to popular belief, vampires could be exposed to sunlight. It hurt. It also drained. But it didn't kill. Unless it was extended, I supposed. I had no real idea. I certainly wasn't going to test that theory – and I didn't know anybody else who was either. I sighed. And unfortunately, unless I wanted to get pulled over every time I hit the road, I couldn't darken the front windshield as much as the other windows.

Thankfully, the sun had almost set by the time I reached Ryan's house. I parallel parked at the curb and walked with almost no pain up to his front door to ring the bell. I smiled when he opened the door and he reflected that back. We held this tableau a hair longer than was comfortable and then we both broke the gaze. Good grief, we were like teenagers.

"Are you ready?"

"Yes, I am," he responded to my back. I was already heading to the car. Once seated, I handed him the lists I received from Catherine.

"She was able to get everything we asked for," I explained excitedly. "We can show the names to Jim, see if he recognizes anybody. We can run the names down ourselves, see if someone has a connection to Jim that he may not be aware of. But first…" I paused.

"It's off to the theater," he finished my statement with an accented dramatic flourish. Actors. We couldn't help ourselves.

We smiled again at each other. I tore my eyes from his lips and faced the road. Get a grip, girl.

CHAPTER SIX

"Hey, Evie," the woman behind the ticket counter called out after we opened the door to the theater.

"Hi, Gail," I responded. Ryan and I approached the desk. "This is Ryan. I don't know if you've met."

"No," Ryan confirmed. "It's nice to meet you, Gail."

"Likewise." Gail looked at me. "What can I do for you guys? Tickets for the weekend?"

"Maybe after. Has Catherine talked to you?"

"No, should she have?"

"Ryan and I are investigating the murder of Monica Freeman."

Gail's eyes widened and she lowered her voice. "Wasn't her husband arrested for that?"

Ryan bristled beside me and I touched his hand to both comfort and silence him. It worked. "Well, we're trying to find out if the right person was arrested."

"Catherine can't stay out of the crime fighting business, can she?" Gail laughed. She was correct, of course; Catherine fell in love with this stuff after her own experiences earlier this year.

I smiled. "No, she can't. She's helping us out. She said we could talk to anybody who was here that night."

"I was here that night," Gail quickly clarified, then frowned. "Although I don't know what I can contribute." Her face brightened. "On the other hand, I can say for certain that Jim and Monica looked very much in love."

"What makes you say that?"

"You know. They kept touching each other. Not in a creepy inappropriate way," she explained with an eye roll. "Just, you know, holding hands, pecks on the lips, that kind of stuff. I was working the ticket counter, like now, so I saw when they arrived, when they got snacks at intermission, and when they left at the end of the night."

"I'm impressed you noticed and remembered all of that," I commented, though secretly I didn't see how she could have. There would have been about one hundred or so people here that night and, frankly, Jim wasn't that memorable. I mean, he's surfer-boy cute, but still.

"Normally I wouldn't have," Gail acknowledged. "They didn't have tickets for the performance, though, and when they came up here to buy them, they were so cute and flirty that I paid attention to them after that. I like happy couples."

Okay, that made sense. I pondered for a moment. "Let's take a different tack. Did anything stand out that night? Anything at all, positive or negative?"

Gail bit her lip while she thought. Ryan and I waited. Tension radiated off his body. He was really putting a lot of stock in this. I felt a smidge of guilt over my ulterior motive and then dismissed it. Either Jim would turn out to be guilty or not. Gail released her lip and smiled uncertainly.

"I'm not sure if it's important. Several people left the theater during intermission. Not just stepped out to smoke, actually left."

This caught my attention. "Why did that stand out? I've seen people leave at intermission before. The show isn't for them."

Gail nodded. "Absolutely. It stood out for two reasons. One, because when a couple of them left, I could really smell the cologne on one of them. It smelled like I was suddenly in a meadow." She chuckled at the memory. "Way overpowering."

"Could the smell also be described as woody?" Ryan asked this with such intensity that Gail's smile faltered in confusion.

"Um, I guess so," she allowed.

Ryan turned to me triumphantly. "There you go."

"Simmer down, big boy," I cautioned him. "It's just a lead."

"No," he argued, "it supports Jim's story."

I could see Gail was lost by this conversation and I also realized I wasn't interested in starting rumors, so I turned to her, effectively cutting off Ryan's train of thought.

"As Ryan says, that's helpful. You said there were two reasons the people leaving at intermission stood out," I prompted.

The redirect worked and Gail focused on me. "Yes! There was this guy. He was dressed like he was going to Broadway. Full tuxedo, the whole nine yards. He looked fabulous."

I frowned and Gail stopped. "No, sorry, it's nothing, please continue." The description reminded me of my ex-husband and I very much wanted to forget him. I pushed the memory away.

"Anyway, he looked great. And irritated. He practically stalked out of here."

"Was he with anyone in particular?"

"Despite the outfit, I somehow missed his arrival. I don't know if he came with someone or not. He seemed to leave alone. Although maybe that was why he looked irritated," she laughed. "Maybe his date didn't go well."

Ah, bad dates. Gail and I shared a girls' moment.

"Could you tell who was the source of the woody smell?"

Gail appeared confused by Ryan's question.

"He's back on the smell you noticed. The meadow, or woody, smell. Could you tell who was wearing the cologne?" I clarified.

"No," she said with a shake of her head. "Sorry, I couldn't." She paused. "Although, I can narrow it down. I smelled it at the beginning of intermission and then it faded."

"Maybe that means it was one of the people who left early?" I finished the thought for her.

"Yes!"

"That's very helpful, thank you, Gail."

We said our goodbyes and continued the tour of questions. Unfortunately, we learned nothing new.

The woman manning the concession area didn't remember Jim and Monica, didn't notice a smell because she had a cold that night, though she did remember a tall, good-looking man in a tuxedo.

Since a pick-up rehearsal was in full swing, the actors from that night were in the theater. Unfortunately, they were even less help. That night had been opening weekend, so they were focused on the show, and they remembered nothing out of the ordinary.

Ryan and I headed back to the car to regroup.

"Now we have a few things to look for when we cull through the lists Catherine gave us," I said.

"And we have confirmation of the woody smell."

"Yes, we do," I agreed.

"What do you think we should do next?"

I was flattered that Ryan thought I knew what I was doing. I had been flying by the seat of my pants the entire time. But, I did have an idea. "I have two thoughts. First, I'll forward you the lists for you to forward to Jim."

"He can read through them and tell us if he recognizes anybody."

"Yep. Though it'll be important for him not to dismiss anyone as a possible suspect; if he recognizes a name, he needs to tell us. Otherwise, we could completely miss something," I warned.

"Makes sense. And second?"

"Time for some internet sleuthing. We split the names up and google all of them. See if anybody pops up as memorable or remarkable in any way. Once we've narrowed the list to those folks, plus anybody who doesn't have an internet footprint—"

"People like that exist?" Ryan quipped.

I laughed and continued. "Then we go visit those people."

Ryan nodded. "Let's go find a murderer."

Or prove they already found him.

CHAPTER SEVEN

Ryan and I approached my condo door. My nerves fluttered. Why on earth was I anxious? It wasn't like I hadn't brought a man home before. Or several dozen – hey, I'd been single for many decades. Still.

I unlocked the door and my hand hesitated before I pushed it open to grant Ryan entry first. I followed behind, focused on the lock, and not on his butt in his jeans. Argh. What was wrong with me?

The man was fine, for sure.

He politely paused inside the door until I flipped the lock and could lead the way.

"Welcome to my humble abode," I announced with a sweep of my arm. I saw his eyes rove as we walked all the way into the condo. I pointed out the various created sections of the condo and his eyes followed my finger.

"Nice place. That view is spectacular."

"Thanks. It's the main reason I bought it," I acknowledged. "Plus, the neighbors are great. It's a colorful building. And, Catherine lives down the hall."

"Catherine Rodham? Our agent?"

"Yep," I nodded, then frowned slightly. "Though, I don't know if that's common knowledge, so don't tell anyone."

"My lips are sealed," he assured me and we shared a smile.

O-kay, time to focus.

"I thought we could work at the table," I explained, gesturing to the rustic wooden dining table. Ryan nodded and began setting up his laptop, while I grabbed mine off my desk to join him. We sat across from each other.

"I'll send the lists to Jim right now." He typed slowly and methodically. He would never win a typing contest.

"Sounds good, let me know the instant he responds back."

"Will do."

"In the meantime, let's divvy up the names we have and start plugging them into Google."

"Sounds good to me. I can start with the season-ticket holders," Ryan offered.

"And I'll start with the credit card pre-sales."

We smiled at each other before focusing on our screens. His long legs managed to bump my average ones enough that part of me wondered if he was doing it on purpose. Could he be playing footsies? Surely not. Probably just a coincidence. Probably.

About forty-five minutes later, I stood to stretch. Internet searching was not that exciting. And so far, we'd come up with bupkis. Nada.

Ryan's eyes lit up. "Email from Jim."

I walked behind him to read over his shoulder. He smelled good, fresh. Ryan opened the email and we scanned Jim's response. Ryan's shoulders slumped. I returned to my seat.

"He only recognizes a few and doesn't think any of them could be involved."

"We'll run them down anyway," I assured him and he half-smiled.

"Thanks."

Ryan and I quickly concurred with Jim's opinion and eliminated the people he knew as suspects. Mainly because we could not for the life of us come up with any motive. That was how we were eliminating almost everybody at this point.

For the season-ticket holders, most of them were older and retired. Why would they want to see Monica dead? For the advanced credit-card sales, that demographic skewed younger, but still we struggled to identify a connection to Jim, let alone a motive. It wasn't until we were reviewing the final list of names, the walk-up day-of credit card sales, that I saw a name that left me nauseous. Not sure how that could happen to a vampire. Curdled the blood still coursing from my pre-dinner drink?

I didn't think the man had a connection to Jim and Monica. He definitely had a connection to me.

"See someone interesting?" Ryan asked this casually but I breathed in sharply. That got his attention. "What is it? Something promising?"

I heard the lift in his voice and I hated to disappoint him. I shook my head and watched his optimism deflate.

"Just a name I hadn't expected to see."

Now he was clearly curious.

I opened my mouth to explain and nothing came out. I was rarely speechless.

"Is everything okay?"

"Why wouldn't it be?" My flippant response seemed mean given the genuine concern I heard in his voice. I didn't know if I could talk about it.

"Ex-boyfriend?"

He offered this as a joke to lighten the mood but he was too close to a bullseye. And he could see that.

"Hey, no worries. You don't have to talk about it." He held up his hands like stop signs. "Unless you want to."

"Um, not ex-boyfriend," I started. "Ex-husband." The phrase squeaked out.

Ryan's eyebrows shot skyward. "Ex-husband? Oh."

"I haven't seen him in … years." I paused. "He doesn't live in Vegas. I don't know why he would have been at the show the night of Monica's murder." He couldn't possibly be involved, could he?

Ryan's eyes narrowed, so my horrible poker face let something slip. "Could he be involved? Is that at all a possibility?" His white knuckles betrayed his tension.

Seeing him grip the side of the dining room table, I realized I had to be at least a little bit forthcoming.

I closed my eyes and gave my head a small positive shake. "Yeah, it's possible. He's not the—" I stopped, unsure what to say. "Yeah, it's possible," I repeated.

"He's our only lead," Ryan said softly. "We need to talk to him."

"I'll find him. I'll talk to him," I responded firmly. "You can chase down these last couple of names we can't account for."

Ryan's expression objected to the arrangement, but he remained quiet.

I checked my watch. "It's just after 11 p.m. Do you have to work tomorrow?"

"Yes," Ryan sighed. "I can try to leave early to work on these five names. What about you?"

"I'll track down my ex and talk to him. We'll touch base once we have the information. Probably tomorrow after work."

Ryan's lips tightened. "I guess that'll have to do."

I smiled hesitantly. "It'll be okay. We'll have a better idea of our next steps tomorrow."

"I hope so. Let me know if you need me." I bit my lower lip and he blushed. "Um, need me to help you handle your ex."

"Oh, him, I'll be fine," I said, unconvincingly.

"Are you sure? If there's a chance he's involved, could he be dangerous? Are you sure you don't want me to come along?"

"Slow down, hero," I said with a grin. "I appreciate the concern. It'll be fine. If I need anything, I'll absolutely reach out," I assured him. This seemed to mollify him at least a little bit.

"Okay. You have my number," he reminded me.

"I know." I reached across the table to rest my hand on his arm. He took my hand in his. We held hands for a long moment. I enjoyed his warmth and the increase in his heart rate. Our eyes met over the table, both of us questioning what we were doing. I released his hand and stood. "I'll walk you out."

He jumped up, knocking the chair against the table. "I guess that's my cue," he responded with a wink.

"That's not what I meant!"

"I know. However, you're right, I do need to get going. Don't you have to work tomorrow?"

I'd been waiting for this question. After decades of investing, I didn't have to work. I was an actress because it was fun, not because I needed the money. However, I wasn't going to say anything to Ryan about that.

"Nope," I said with a quick shake of my head. "Just waiting to hear from Catherine about my next audition." I saw his curiosity about my ability to afford this condo and, well, life, without a regular gig. Vegas had a low cost of living, but it wasn't free. He said nothing though and we walked to the door. I opened it and he hesitated.

"Thanks again for helping me with this," he said softly.

"Of course. Like I said before, I believe in truth." Even painful truth. Although the more time I spent with Ryan, the more I hoped I might be wrong. Imagining how crushed he would be to get confirmation that Jim was actually the killer pained me.

On the other hand, maybe he needed to learn that lesson. You couldn't trust people. My ex-husband being in town was yet more proof of that.

"Goodnight Ryan." I wondered for a moment if he was going to kiss me, the energy between us pulsed so strong. His eyes dilated and we stared a moment. I broke eye contact first.

"Goodnight, Evie. I'll talk to you tomorrow." He leaned in for a hug – man, he felt good – and then he was gone, taking his heat with him. I watched him walk to the elevator for a moment, enjoying the view. He turned to offer a half-wave, caught the line of my gaze and wolfishly grinned. My face flushed, and I laughed before closing the door. I could hear him chuckling. The elevator doors pinged.

If I had a heartbeat, it'd be racing, I'm sure.

I leaned against the door, breathing deeply. Strictly speaking, I didn't need to breathe. I could force air in and out my lungs, though, and some habits were ingrained. Even after all these years, I found deep breathing calming, even if biologically it did nothing for me.

Shaking off the impact of Ryan and his departure, I strode to my bedroom. Time to change clothing.

If Derek was in town, he'd be hitting the nightclubs.

CHAPTER EIGHT

After flaming out at the typical nightclubs, I struck pay dirt. I stood at the bar, vibrating to the pulsing music, scanning the dancefloor through the fake fog and laser lights. Other vampires surrounded me. I drank an AB-negative cocktail – it was expensive because it was the rarest but, man, did it taste sweet.

And then I spotted him. Derek stood out wherever he went. The tallest man in the room, with a very flamboyant style. He was holding court with a bevy of beauties, also not uncommon for him. Since he hadn't seen me yet, I took a moment to consider him.

Derek Smith. Yes, that was his real last name. He kept it all these years because it was so ordinary. At 6'5" tall, with black hair, eyes so brown they appeared black, and alabaster skin, wearing black leather pants that showed every contour and a white button-down shirt with the first three buttons undone, he looked like a rock star. I watched him with a mixture of appreciation for his frozen-in-time good looks and revulsion for his complete amorality. Not that the vamps around him cared.

Eventually, he registered that someone outside that cooing group of, well, groupies, was aware of him. He looked around with a seductive smile, trying to identify if the person watching was more important or better looking than the women around him. I observed the change in his expression when our eyes met.

Good grief, he looked happy to see me. Really? After everything?

Derek made a beeline for me, to the consternation of the women, who immediately started casing for a replacement.

"Why are you in town?" was my caustic greeting. I had zero interest in being nice to this narcissist.

"To see you, of course," he responded in a low voice, likely intended to go with the seductive look. As if any of that worked on me.

I rolled my eyes and his smile dropped a bit. "Not likely," I retorted. "Why are you really in town?"

He moved closer and I caught a whiff of something. And then it was absorbed by the multitude of other smells in the nightclub.

"No, really, I am," he insisted, reaching a hand out to touch my cheek. He frowned when I jerked away from his touch. "Now, now, is that any way to greet your husband?"

"Ex," I hissed. "Don't touch me. I'll ask one more time. Why are you really here?"

Derek took a step back and held his arms open wide. "I really am here to win you back. I've missed you. The other reason I'm here is to film a movie."

"Film a movie? Since when are you in the movie business?"

He winked. "I was bored. I got involved with some guys. I'm financing their movie."

"You're a producer?" I asked this with a hint of irritation. He was poaching in my territory now.

"Yep," he answered with a grin. "It's fun. I provide the money, so I'm in charge. And I'm surrounded by beautiful actresses."

I rolled my eyes again, which was not lost on him.

"Hey, until I get you back, a vampire's got to have a little fun."

I mirthlessly laughed. "You do you. But, since apparently decades of experience have yet to sink in. There is zero chance you will ever get me back. Zero," I added for emphasis, since he apparently could add delusional to his list of zany attributes.

He looked wounded. "I've changed, Evie. I finally see what I've done wrong. And I want to do better. For you. For us."

He sounded so earnest. Someone without my years of experience likely would fall for it.

"Stop, Derek. You're embarrassing yourself."

Derek's eyes narrowed. I knew that would strike a chord and I was right.

"Don't be like that." He smoothed out his face. "I'm just being friendly."

"Sure. Whatever," I responded flippantly. I didn't know if he was here to produce a movie or to get me back, or some other reason he had not disclosed. Since he seemed to have been at the theater the night Jim and Monica were attacked, I needed to focus on my purpose in seeking him out to begin with – it certainly wasn't to verbally spar with him until I wanted to vomit.

"Fine," I said with a nicer tone. "What have you been doing since you've been in town?"

He appeared surprised by my conciliatory tone but went with it. I supposed because it fit in with his unshakable belief that he was irresistible. "A little of this and a little of that."

"That sounds fun," was my sarcastic response. "Any new clubs, shows, anything like that?"

My sly attempt to ask about the theater worked and he blathered on about the things he had been doing. I was only half-listening, waiting for something useful in the litany of descriptions of females he'd been with. And then he said what I'd been waiting for.

"And I went to this show at the Las Vegas Independent Theatre."

"Oh, what show did you see?"

He frowned. "I don't remember the name. It wasn't very memorable." He laughed.

"You watched an entire show yet can't remember the name of it." I tried for a teasing tone because his response could be critical.

"Not an entire show," he corrected me. "I left at intermission. Because it was so bad," he clarified.

"I gathered that, Captain Obvious." He frowned, so I hurriedly continued. "You know, I had friends who went to see that show."

"Oh yeah." It was clear he didn't care.

"Maybe you saw them? Either that night or later on the news. Jim and Monica. They were attacked that night in their home."

"Wow, that's terrible. I don't remember meeting anybody with those names."

Most humans would not have noticed the subtle change on Derek's face, it came and went so quickly. Except, I wasn't a human. And, I had history with the man. He knew something, I was sure of it.

"You didn't see anything about it on the news?" I pushed a little.

"No, I didn't. I don't watch the news." His answer was curt and his look more glacial and less seductive now.

I definitely hit a nerve. He smiled suddenly. "I have to go," he said, gesturing vaguely behind him. "I'll be in touch. I told you why I'm really here. This isn't over."

No, it most definitely was not, I silently told his back while he walked away from me. Not by a long shot. And not just because he clearly knew something. Also because I got another whiff of the *something* from earlier. A woody scent. Like Jim smelled the night of the murder.

CHAPTER NINE

Are you awake?

I sent the text to Catherine, chuckling a little. This was getting to be a habit. But, I needed her help again. Besides, it was only just after midnight. I was sure she was awake.

Yep. Come on over.

Smiling, I exited my convertible and headed for the parking garage elevator. In mere minutes, I stood in front of Catherine's door, knocking.

She answered with a smile. "This is getting to be a habit," she joked.

"Did you read my mind?"

Shaking her head with a laugh, she held the door open for me to enter. I walked straight for the couch. I stared at the Las Vegas skyline for a beat while Catherine sat next to me, tucking her legs under her.

"What can I do to help?"

"First, thank you again for getting me the lists of the patrons for the theater."

She waved this off. "Of course. You know, anything I can do to help." She stared at me pointedly.

"Second," I continued with a laugh, "Ryan and I eliminated almost everybody on the lists. He has five names we couldn't truly account for, so he's going to knock those out after work tomorrow. I mean, later today. That still doesn't account for any cash buyers," I said with a single-shoulder shrug, "but there's nothing we can do about them anyway. Plus," I said slowly, "we have a new lead."

Catherine heard the change in my voice. "Who? Is it someone we know?"

"Someone I knew," I answered, unable to disguise the bitterness. Catherine knew I was a vampire. She didn't know my story. That wasn't about to change tonight.

"Who?" she asked again, worried now.

I sighed dramatically, deliberately, trying to ease the tension. "My ex-husband."

"Your ex-husband? I didn't know you had been married."

"It was a long time ago. A long, long, *long* time ago," I added for emphasis.

"Oh, I get it. He's a vampire?"

"Yep."

"How can I help then?"

I silently thanked her for not asking additional questions. "His name is Derek Smith. And, yes, before you ask, that was his human name too. Smith makes a good alias, but some people really did – do – have that as their name." I smiled and she laughed. "He says he's here to produce a movie. Some kind of paranormal thing about vampires." Her eyes widened and she jumped up, startling me.

"I got an email about something like that," she called over her shoulder while she headed for her desk. I turned in my seat to watch her flip open the laptop and start tapping. "Yes, here it is. The working title is *Vampire Nights*. That's creative," she said as an aside. "Anyway, they're seeking actor submissions. Oh, now I get it." She realized why I was there. "You want me to submit you for an audition?"

"Me and Ryan," I amended. "I'm certain I'll get an audition, but I'd like to try to get Ryan on set."

"How are you so certain you'll get the audition?" she asked, lasering in on me when she returned to the couch.

I avoided eye contact. "Derek says he isn't here only for the movie."

"And?"

I sighed. "He says he's here to win me back." I snorted and Catherine laughed.

"Is that a possibility?"

My jaw dropped at the question. "Ugh, not at all. Derek and I have a—" I paused. "Complicated history," I finished. "There is no chance I'd take him back."

"Then you must want on the set for another reason?"

"I tracked Derek to an underground paranormal nightclub earlier tonight. That's when he told me about the movie and wanting to win me back. But, there was more," I said excitedly. "One, I've known him too long. I know he was hiding something. Two, he smelled woody. Exactly like Jim said his house smelled."

"Do you think Derek is the killer?" Catherine appeared confused and I couldn't blame her.

"Honestly, I don't know what to think. Derek has no motive that I can guess, at this point anyway. Jim still looks like the most likely suspect. On the other hand, Derek is hiding something and smelled like Jim described. On the other, other hand," I said with a smile, "playing devil's advocate. If Jim smelled the scent at the theater and not really in the house, that would be a good non-clue to provide to try to throw people off the, um, scent, so to speak."

Catherine chuckled at my statement but nodded. "Yeah, any of that could be the case. I can see why you want to be on set."

"Time to put my detective skills to work," I said, rubbing my hands together like an excited child.

"You have detective skills?" Catherine asked this and I threw a pillow at her. I rose to leave before she could kick me out, and we both paused when a tentative knock sounded at her door.

"Robin, what can I do for you?" Catherine asked the woman standing on the other side of her open door. She pitched her voice pleasant but not exactly welcoming. I stood a few steps behind her and wondered about Robin's presence.

I knew about Catherine's encounters during the serial murders last spring with Robin Landon – and the woman who pulled her marionette strings, Councilwoman Barbara Knollman.

"I'm glad I caught you both here," the slight woman began, and I laughed. She frowned at me.

"You showed up unannounced in the middle of the night – in a building with 24-hour security – without knowing we were here? Please," Catherine snorted derisively.

Robin ignored our rudeness and continued speaking, voice smooth. "A certain interested party is aware that the two of you are investigating the Monica Freeman murder—"

"We know you work for the Councilwoman," Catherine mumbled and I didn't have to see her face to know she did a hard eye roll. I'd had enough of this cloak and dagger nonsense.

"You mean the demon," I corrected Catherine and her mouth dropped open. Robin looked nonplussed. "Oh yeah, I guess you didn't know," I added with a wide smile. I stepped in front of Catherine. "And, our girl here is officially a minion."

Robin bristled at the word, eyes glittering angrily. "That's offensive."

"I'm not too politically correct about demons," I retorted. I could hear Catherine spluttering to herself behind me about demons. I turned and placed my hand on her arm and made eye contact.

"I'm a vampire and you're dating a half-incubus; can you really be so surprised that the head of the city council is a demon with minions?"

Catherine shrugged a shoulder. "When you put it that way…" She and I turned to face Robin. "What does the Councilwoman want?" Catherine asked.

"She has a vested interest in your investigation."

My eyes narrowed. "Why?"

"I'm not at liberty to say."

I laughed. "Probably because you don't actually know," I responded, meaner than normal. I'd never liked the minion. I sighed. "Apologies for my rudeness," I backtracked. "Do you have a specific question for me or Catherine?"

Catherine's mouth dropped open again at my conciliatory tone and offer to answer questions. She hadn't learned yet; Barbara Knollman was easier to handle if you let her have the small things.

"We know Catherine gave you theater patron lists. We also know that you and Derek were seen out together tonight. What is his involvement in the murder?"

I inwardly cringed. Of course, this was really about Derek. "We don't know yet," I answered honestly. "What does Barbara want with him?"

"I'll let the councilwoman know," Robin responded to my statement and ignored my question; she inclined her head slightly and then turned silently to head toward the elevator.

"What was that about?" Catherine asked once the elevator door closed and Robin began her downward descent.

"I don't know, but we need to have a talk with security about letting just anybody up here without calling first."

Catherine's barked laugh held a note of hysteria in it. I closed her door and placed a hand on her shoulder.

"Everything okay?"

She opened and closed her mouth a couple of times, processing. "You're correct I'm aware of the supernatural underworld, including vampires and incubi," she enunciated slowly. "But, demons with actual minions?"

The high pitch of her voice asking that question worried me and I hugged her.

"Catherine? An incubus is a demon, remember? Like Alex, your half-incubus boyfriend?"

She nodded. "Can you explain the demon and minion thing again?"

"I don't know much, except that the councilwoman showed up a couple of decades ago. She quickly ascended to running things, on the council and in the paranormal world." I waved a hand dismissively. "I don't think she's high in the demon hierarchy—"

"Demon hierarchy?"

"Um, yeah, I think that's what it's called. Vampires don't really get involved in the political stuff. Well, the heads of vampire families do," I corrected myself. "That's not me." I smiled.

"What about Robin?"

"She does the councilwoman's bidding. Which you already knew. I don't know her story."

Catherine nodded and took a ragged breath. "Okay."

I hugged her again. "I wish I knew their interest in the murder and my ex-husband."

CHAPTER TEN

I checked my phone after I completed recharging the next evening. A flurry of texts awaited. Most were from Catherine and Ryan. I ignored the lift I felt seeing Ryan's name. Get it together. This wasn't a romantic comedy.

I was pleased to see Catherine had confirmed the auditions. Oh shoot, they were tonight. I texted her back, thanking her again, and assuring her that I'd be there.

Ryan sent several texts.

12:30 p.m. *Catherine says I have an audition tonight. Did you get one too?*

1:30 p.m. *I just noticed that the producer's name is Derek. Is that your ex?*

3:30 p.m. *Is everything okay? Did anything happen last night?*

4:30 p.m. *The audition is tonight at 7p. If you weren't invited, maybe you can still crash it. Text or call me…*

It was 5:19 p.m. now. I felt bad Ryan had been worried, and maybe a little happy he'd been thinking of me. I texted him back immediately.

Hey Ryan! Sorry for the delay in responding. Got in late and slept most of the day :) Yes, Catherine sent me the same text. And, yes, that's my ex. I'll explain when I pick you up in an hour. I assume you'd like a ride to the audition?

Ryan must have had his phone right next to him. I received a response before I could even place the cellphone back on the side table. I was still in bed and needed to get up to prepare for the audition.

So glad to hear from you. Yes, would love a ride to the audition. Def curious to know how your ex is involved…

I deliberately ignored the unasked question in the text since I already told Ryan he'd hear all about it in the car.

Sounds good. See you soon!

Ryan responded with a thumbs-up emoji and now I knew I could set the phone down to get ready. Choosing what outfit to wear was a bit of a dilemma. I was confident Derek would cast me regardless, if he was telling the truth that his agenda was to win me back, though I shuddered at that. I didn't want to mislead him in any way, shape, or form by dressing sexy. But I couldn't really wear a burlap sack to an audition.

I sighed and chose to go with my standard audition outfit: dark blue jeans, green t-strap heels, pale green crepe de chine embroidered short-sleeve blouse over a spaghetti strap camisole, with a matching cloche hat. Although consisting of replicas, this outfit, except the jeans, was so reminiscent of my 1920s clothing that I always felt the most comfortable in it. Hence why I wore it to auditions. Even if I didn't need the money, every actress wanted to be cast.

I carefully applied my natural makeup and dark red lipstick. Contrary to popular belief, most women in the 1920s did not do their makeup crazy heavy like in the movies. Other than the red lips, we kept it pretty light and basic.

I texted Ryan to let him know I was on my way. A short time later, I pulled into his driveway. I started to exit the vehicle when his front door opened. I pulled my door closed and watched him walk toward me. Man, he looked good. He'd opted for a blue short-sleeve knit top and dark blue jeans with, I think, brown boots. He looked good enough to eat. Well, not like that. I didn't drink fresh human blood, remember?

Ryan's pupils dilated when he entered the car and I knew it was a case of mutual admiration. The sexual tension in the car rolled around the enclosed space, nearly overwhelming; he coughed. Nervously. I heard his heartbeat accelerating.

I smiled. He smiled back. And just like that, the tension dissipated. For the time being at least.

"I'm glad you got the audition too," Ryan started off, then made a face. "Although, I'm guessing you were a slam dunk for it, right?"

"Yeah."

"Are you responsible for my audition too?"

"Yes and no," I answered truthfully. "I asked Catherine to submit you for it, yes. Though, she likely would have anyway. And neither of us had any control over whether or not Derek would select you to audition."

"Wouldn't he have a casting director to do that?"

I nodded. "Oh sure, but I have no doubt that he's the one calling the shots. He's a bit of a control freak." This was a massive understatement.

"Hmm. Okay," Ryan responded, looking like he wanted to ask a follow up question. Interestingly, he chose not to. "I'm glad we both get to go. Tell me why it's so important that we do. Is it related to Jim and Monica?"

"It seems to be," I hedged.

"What happened last night?" His face pinched like he was choking on a sour lemon when he asked this and I laughed.

"I'm sorry to laugh, but you should see yourself. Trust me, I did not enjoy talking to Derek. I finally tracked him down and we had a mercifully brief conversation. He explained that he's in town doing this movie. I could tell he was hiding something."

"How?"

"It's just something you learn after knowing somebody for so long," I answered with a non-answer. "The reason I think he may know something was his smell. He smelled woody."

"Exactly like Jim described." Ryan thought for a moment. "Do you think he could be the killer?"

"Honestly, I don't know. I have no idea what his motive would be." I chose not to share the alternative theory that Jim smelled the scent at the theater and was using it for misdirection. I was fairly confident that Ryan would not be receptive to this theory. "The only way to find out more is to be around him; the movie set is the easiest way to do that naturally."

"I agree. Good thinking."

"Let's head on over then." I headed toward the strip mall location of the audition. "One more thing," I said with as offhand a tone as I could muster. "When we get there, you should go in ahead of me and we should act like we don't know each other."

"Why?"

"If we're going to be poking around on set, we need to make sure that we both get cast and it's best that he not know we're together." I had a feeling this partial answer would not be satisfactory.

"And, I ask again, why?" He sounded genuinely perplexed.

"We don't want him to know we're investigating him," I answered, and it sounded lame even to my own ears.

"That doesn't make any sense," Ryan argued. "People in this town know and talk to each other at auditions and on set all the time. There would be no reason for him to suspect that we're investigating him."

A quick glance in his direction showed me his eyes had narrowed.

"What aren't you telling me?"

Asked a direct question, I refused to lie. I sighed instead. "When I talked with Derek yesterday, he said he had an ulterior motive for getting involved with this movie." I paused and Ryan waited for me to continue.

"And?" He prompted me with the question after a long silence.

I rolled my eyes. "Ugh, he says he wants to win me back." I heard Ryan's heartbeat accelerate and knew he did not like this news.

"Really," was all he said.

"He has no chance," I assured Ryan, though was unsure why I cared so much. Yes, we obviously were attracted to each other. But, we were focused on clearing Jim's name. Well, Ryan was. The jury was still out on that for me.

"He doesn't?"

"Not. At. All."

Ryan laughed, low and sexy. "Good."

I saw the two-story building ahead and used that as the perfect distraction to the tension.

"We're here," I announced cheerily. I pulled into a parking spot and killed the engine. I turned to face Ryan, who had done the same. "You go in first. I'll wait five minutes. Then I'll go in."

"And you're sure this is necessary?"

"Trust me. It's much easier this way. If Derek thinks we're together, you'll never get cast. I can promise you that."

Ryan shook his head. "Okay. I'll see you inside."

He exited the vehicle and I watched his backside while he entered the ground floor storefront. Dang, the man looked good coming and going.

68

CHAPTER ELEVEN

Exactly five minutes later, I swung open my car door and prepared to snoop, I mean, audition. Once inside the building, I saw a young woman behind a desk and a few people sitting on chairs around the room. I avoided looking at Ryan. Everyone held audition sides, preparing.

"Hi, you're here to audition," the cheerful woman behind the desk stated. I idly wondered if she was a production assistant or casting assistant.

"Yes," I confirmed.

"Please sign in and take the appropriate sides for the character you'd like to audition for," she instructed, indicating a clipboard and two rows of single sheets of paper.

I signed-in on the appropriate line, noting Ryan's was the only one above me. That was bad. If there was a side with a couple, we might end up auditioning together.

Derek wasn't stupid. His animal instincts were strong; he'd notice the sexual tension. I quickly reviewed the available sides and saw that, unfortunately, there was only one character I was right for. The romantic lead. I sighed and snatched the side off the table.

I sat on a hard, plastic chair, reading over the selected scene's dialogue. A young man came through a door next to the reception desk. He checked the clipboard and called out the name before Ryan's. I gave Derek credit; at least the audition was running smoothly. It was such a crap shoot in this town, pun intended. Some auditions, you were in and out within thirty minutes. Others, the ones we described as *cattle calls* in the industry, could result in hours of waiting. Those sucked.

The owner of the name followed the young man and five minutes later returned. Checking the clipboard, the young man called out Ryan's name and he disappeared behind the door. Five minutes later, they both came out. Except that, instead of leaving, Ryan retook his seat. Shoot. Sometimes I hated when I was right.

The young man, who smelled like a vampire, I realized, called my name. He introduced himself as Orlando. I smiled broadly, confirmed my identity, and followed him through the door. We walked down a short hallway to a larger room. There was an X on the floor, a camera on a tripod five feet in front of it, and four people sitting in a ragged half-circle behind the camera.

"Evelyn Jones," the young vampire announced and then faded into the background.

This obviously wasn't my first time at an audition. I handed my headshot and resume to the person holding her hand out, and walked over to the big X. I was curious to see how Derek handled this. He sat closest to the camera, watched me through dark eyes.

"Hi, Evie," Derek called out. "So glad you could make it to the audition."

I smiled my biggest, fakest, actress smile at him. "Of course. Glad to be here, Derek."

"Show us what you got," he encouraged, "though I know you got it." He winked lecherously at me and I was pleased I refrained from gagging in response. The others in the room, not understanding the undercurrent, chuckled like the sycophants they likely were. Newbie vampires. Ugh.

I performed the side as requested. The woman sitting beside Derek gave a redirect. I performed the side again. Everyone smiled.

"Thanks for coming in, Evie. If you'll wait out front, we'll have you read with one or two of the other actors," Derek said.

"Of course, thank you." Then I was back in the waiting room. The occupants had dwindled to me, Ryan, and another couple. My guess was I'd read with each of the men. And I was right. Soon, only Ryan and I remained in the waiting area. We'd done a good job ignoring each other, but I was a little anxious about how reading with him would go.

Orlando entered the room. "Evelyn and Ryan? We're ready for you."

Ryan and I looked at each other, smiled at the vampire, and followed him back through the door. Here went nothing. Or everything.

The female vampire I previously handed my headshot to indicated where Ryan and I should stand. "From the top," Derek intoned dramatically, and we began.

I stared into Ryan's eyes, embodying the words I was reading. So did he. His voice was husky, his eyes dilated as we read. I mirrored his physicality. He was good. We went through the entire scene. I'll admit it helped doing a romantic scene when you were already attracted to someone. We finished and remained staring at each other, for a beat too long apparently. Someone coughed.

We tore our eyes from each other and looked out at the half circle. I noticed with mild alarm that Derek now wore a half-frown. The female vampire, however, was smiling.

"That was fantastic," she crowed.

"Yes," Derek slowly agreed. "That was quite good." His eyes narrowed. "Have the two of you worked together before?"

"No," we responded in unison, and I inwardly sighed. The answer was true, but who spoke at the same time? Couples did, that's who.

The expression on Derek's face hardened at our response and I realized I needed to do something now or the plan would be over before it started.

"No," I repeated, "but it'll be nice working with *you*." I hated the saccharine tone in my voice and sensed Ryan tensing beside me. However, the ploy worked. Derek focused fully on me, a seductive smile curving upward.

"Yes, yes, it will," he agreed. I channeled every ounce of my inner actress to maintain my mildly flirtatious expression and attitude.

"When will we get the good news we've been cast?"

"We?"

I heard the alpha male in Derek's voice. Dang it, he was so sensitive. "Oh, come on, Derek," I said breezily. "My reading with—" I paused and looked questioningly at Ryan.

"Ryan," he supplied, suppressing a small smile.

"My reading with Ryan was better than with the other guy. Unless you plan on callbacks because you saw someone fantastic earlier this evening, it has to be us."

Derek laughed. "My little minx."

I cringed internally at the word, but outwardly did the cutesy eyes downcast thing that certain men seemed to respond to.

"We'll review all the tape and let agents know by the end of the week," he answered my earlier question.

We made eye contact again and I fought down the revulsion to continue the charade. Miraculously, it worked. "That's wonderful," I purred. The female vampire rolled her eyes and I wondered how often scenes like this played out between Derek and actresses. Despite his expressed intent to win me back, I suspected this happened all the time.

The female vampire stood, smiled broadly at Ryan. Her smile dimmed slightly when directed at me. "Thank you both for coming in. We'll let you know."

Ryan and I echoed her thanks and then began to leave.

"Evie, can you stay a minute?"

I immediately stopped. Ryan wisely chose to keep going, like he didn't hear Derek's question. I could tell by Ryan's physical reaction that he did, and he wasn't happy. I'd deal with that later. I turned to Derek.

"Of course."

The other vampires scattered, presumably to give Derek and me privacy. Ugh. He approached and I plastered my big fake grin on again.

"That was fun," I told him. That part was true; I enjoyed reading with Ryan.

Derek touched my cheek and I was impressed I didn't flinch away. "You're so beautiful."

"Thank you," I responded, though my words sounded stiff to my own ears and I was unsurprised to see his smile dip.

"I told you why I'm in town. Yet you still auditioned. And you're here today pretending to flirt. Why are you really here?"

Uh-oh. A direct question. I needed an answer that wasn't a lie. An omission, by the way, was not a lie. "I really want to do the film," I answered, and I was somewhat surprised to realize that was true. The script sounded fun and even though I wasn't sure how Derek became a part of it, the production company was legit, according to Catherine.

Derek stared at me, as though trying to read my mind. He smiled. "I believe you. And you were flirting just so you could get cast?"

"Yes," I admitted, feeling sleazy, hearing it said aloud.

Derek laughed uproariously. "There was no need. Once I knew you were auditioning, I planned to cast you in the lead. You didn't have to flirt." He took my hand. "Though I enjoyed that you did. How far do you want to go with it?" His voice lowered and his eyes were liquid desire. Oh no, no, no.

I snatched my hand away. "Not that far," I retorted and his expression hardened again. The vampire really didn't like not getting his way. Sheesh. I smiled to soften the blow. I didn't want to screw this up in the home stretch. "Let's take this one day at a time."

Derek returned my smile, reached out to caress my cheek again. "Okay. I can understand why you'd be hesitant. We'll take it one day at a time."

His quick acquiescence surprised me before I realized he knew it was the smart play. "I'll see you on set, then," I stated, effectively ending the conversation.

He knew what I did, shook his head slightly. "See you then."

He walked away. I stood there for a long moment, trying to unfeel the touch of his fingers on my face. He hadn't touched me like that in decades. I hadn't missed it.

I spun on my heels and headed outside for the expected showdown with Ryan.

CHAPTER TWELVE

Ryan materialized out of the dark the instant I left the building. Before he could open his mouth, I quietly directed him otherwise.

"The car, first. We don't want anyone here to see us together, remember?"

He followed the instruction and quickly put about ten feet of distance between us. We met again at the car, opened the doors, took our seats, and slammed the doors shut, all in about ten seconds. Ryan remained quiet until we pulled out of the parking lot.

I sensed the tension rolling off of him and waited for the challenge. In three, two, one…

"What was that about back there?" Ryan asked, trying and failing to keep the question light.

"What do you mean?" I questioned back, even though I knew exactly what he meant.

"You know what I'm asking. What was up with the flirting? I thought you didn't like your ex."

"Oh, come on, Ryan," I responded, exasperated. "You're a smart man. You have to know why I was flirting with Derek."

Silence greeted my statement. I waited him out. The silence stretched through one traffic light and then a second. I still waited him out.

"Okay," he said.

"Okay?"

"You're right. I did know why you were flirting with him. To make sure you were cast."

"We," I corrected.

"What?"

"To make sure *we* were cast."

Ryan smiled. "Right. To make sure we were cast."

"Derek suspected we knew each other. I mean, he flat out asked us if we'd worked together before. That would have been a dangerous road to go down."

"That's true. I guess I'm still not clear why that would have been such a big deal. If we had worked together before."

I hesitated to answer. I heard irritation in his voice again and I was unsure if I should address it; Ryan surely felt the sexual tension between us. Right?

"It's not like we're a couple or anything," Ryan continued when I didn't respond.

I didn't like his statement, so for misdirection, I agreed with him.

"That's certainly true," I said with a forced chuckle. "But, I know my ex. He's a classic alpha male."

Ryan laughed. "I got that impression." His expression sobered. "Still."

"Still, what?"

"I don't know," he admitted. He paused to collect his thoughts. "It still felt like you were playing both sides," he finally allowed.

That shocked me. "What? What does that even mean?"

"That maybe you're using our mission as an excuse to explore the possibility of getting back together with your ex."

My jaw dropped open and I risked a glance at him. I noted the clenched jaw and rigid posture. "Are you kidding?"

"Do I look like I'm kidding?"

"No, you don't. And I have no idea why you're overreacting like this." I was facing forward again and I heard the rustle of his clothing when he shifted in the seat to look at me.

"You think I'm overreacting?"

He asked this with a genuine question in his voice. I looked at him and nodded. "Yes, I do. What I don't understand is why."

Silence again. I assumed Ryan was deciding how, or whether, he wanted to answer what I was asking. I had taken the highway exit to his neighborhood when he sighed deeply.

"Did I tell you I was married too?" He said this almost sheepishly because he already knew the answer. "I didn't," he answered himself.

Somehow, I was not surprised. "And?"

"We married young. We were married for five years. I don't think either one of us knew how to be married."

"It's a learning curve for everyone, I think."

"I honestly thought love would be enough. If she was ever really in love with me." He paused. "I didn't know it until the last year that she cheated on me almost every chance she got. I don't know how I missed it."

"Trust me, cheaters know how to cover their tracks," I assured him.

Out of the corner of my eye, I saw Ryan's head turn toward me again. His expression was almost accusatory.

"I never cheated on my husband," I defensively responded to his look.

Ryan sighed again. "Sorry, I'm projecting."

"Projecting?" That was a therapy word if I'd ever heard one.

"I was in therapy for the last six months of my marriage," he said as if reading my mind.

"Ah," was all I could think of to say.

"My best friend saw her out with her latest boyfriend and he finally told me," he continued. "I didn't believe him. I said some horrible things. Lost the friendship," Ryan said, muted anguish audible in his voice.

"I'm sorry."

"When I first questioned Maureen, she called my friend a liar and denied it."

"Of course."

"But, when I provided the details of what my friend had seen, she spilled it all. That's when I learned the current one was only the latest of a string of men. She had been cheating since we returned from our honeymoon," Ryan stated in a flat voice.

"Wow." I was clearly a brilliant conversationalist, but I honestly didn't know what to say.

"After six months of therapy – alone, since she told me she cheated because she should never have gotten married in the first place – I finally filed for divorce. That was five years ago. I haven't dated anybody seriously since then. I guess you could say I have trust issues," he finished with a shake of his head.

"Now I understand." And I truly did. He clearly didn't want to acknowledge any attraction between us, but he knew it was there, so when I flirted with Derek, his subconscious really did interpret that as *playing both sides* like he accused.

"I'm glad. What about you?"

Oh dang. Here came the expectation of reciprocity. I considered and discarded the option of telling him my ex-husband was also my sire and then wiping his mind of the conversation when we got to his house. "Derek and I were married for a short time. It didn't work out and I haven't seen him in a while." Like decades.

A total pregnant pause followed my statement while Ryan waited for me to elaborate. Luckily, I was saved from having to give an even less helpful explanation.

"We've arrived at your home," I announced unnecessarily when I pulled into his driveway. "Door to door service."

Ryan stared at me for a beat before opening his car door. His disappointment in my failure to be equally forthcoming was etched across his face. "I'll see you on set."

"Looking forward to it," I responded with a smile he did not return.

He exited the car, then leaned back in. "Oh, by the way, none of the names on that list panned out. Derek remains our only suspect in Monica's murder." He closed the door.

"And Jim," I told the empty car while I watched Ryan walk to his door. He let himself in without a backward glance.

CHAPTER THIRTEEN

Having hit a roadblock investigating Monica's murder, the next few days passed in a blur with no real contact with Ryan. I knew I found him attractive. I was shocked by how much I missed him. Our limited contact consisted of: me checking in with him after Catherine informed me we had been cast, me asking him if he wanted to rehearse the scenes for the weekend, and his curt responses to my texts. I could read between the lines. He was clearly still upset I hadn't told him anything about my marriage. At least I'd finally see him tonight, since it would be our first day on the set of *Vampire Nights*. He didn't ask for a ride, and I didn't offer, but he couldn't avoid me on set.

All thoughts of Ryan and solving Monica's murder fled on set. I arrived at the house being used for the opening scenes and immediately saw that something was wrong. The degree of excitement and activity was way lower than normal for a first day of shooting. Nothing looked set up yet – no lights, sound equipment, nothing. I placed my bag on the floor of a dining room off the front door and approached Orlando, the young male vampire from the audition, my kitten heels clicking on the laminate floor.

"What's going on?"

He looked at me for a moment, as though distracted from deep thoughts and was now trying to place me. "Oh, Evelyn! Good to see you," he gushed, though even this was forced, off somehow.

"What's going on?" I asked again.

He stared at me. It was obvious he didn't want to answer my question. I could almost see his brain thinking. He sighed.

"Several of our crew members aren't here," he replied vaguely.

"Do they have an estimated arrival time?" I asked this to determine if the shoot would be cancelled, but also to get at what the vampire clearly didn't want to tell me.

He leaned in closer. "Promise not to tell anyone?"

What were we, in high school? I played along. I leaned in too. "I promise."

"Derek isn't here either. A body has been found," he finished dramatically.

If I had a beating heart, it would have stopped. "A body? Whose? Where?"

"I don't know," he answered with a shake of his head. "It wasn't somebody connected directly to the shoot, but our director, camera guy, and hair and makeup chick, all called in this morning. Apparently, they normally work together, and all three know the woman who was killed."

This caught my attention. "Woman?"

"Yes, she was beaten to death. Bludgeoned, really," he said with a level of glee that reminded me how inhumane some non-humans truly could be.

"Why isn't Derek here? How is he connected?" I tried to ask this offhandedly, but I was keenly aware that Derek was the only suspect in Monica's murder besides Jim. Could he be connected to this murder too? That would be quite the coincidence.

"I don't know. All I know is that he got a phone call an hour ago, made a few more phone calls, and then took off after telling me what I just told you."

I didn't know what to make of this information. I clearly needed to find out more.

"Has Ryan arrived yet?" I asked, and Orlando didn't follow my train of thought.

"Um, yeah, he's over talking to wardrobe." He waved his hand to indicate somewhere toward the back of the house.

"Thanks," I told him and headed that way. I stopped short in the doorway of a back room.

Ryan's auburn hair glowed from the floor lamp behind him. Like fire. Oh, good grief, there I went again, thinking like a romance novel. But, man, he looked good, in a simple pair of jeans and a green t-shirt showcasing his fit body. Our eyes met and for just a moment, he seemed glad to see me, and then a wall crashed down behind his eyes.

Pretending obliviousness, I approached Ryan and the costumer, a short round older male with an easy smile. He gave me the up and down, not lasciviously, but with an eye for wardrobe. He nodded his head in approval at my blond bob, yellow pedal-pusher pants, and daisy accented blouse.

"Hi, I'm Jackson. You must be Evelyn and you are absolutely radiant. Like a ray of sunshine," he greeted me, extending his hand. He had a strong grip.

"Thank you so much and nice to meet you, Jackson. Please, call me Evie," I responded. "Hi, Ryan."

"Hi, Evie."

Jackson's head swiveled between me and Ryan; he sensed the tension, I assumed. I jumped right in. "Do you guys know if the shoot is still happening?"

Ryan frowned. "Why wouldn't it? We were only told there'd be a couple of hours delay. Something about an equipment issue."

"Oh, I must have misunderstood," I backtracked with a short bark of a laugh. "Don't let me interrupt."

I tuned the men out and they continued their conversation. My mind raced. How could I find out more information about this murder? It wasn't someone on this set, but someone with a strong connection to the crew. I wondered if Catherine would know.

"Excuse me, gentlemen, I need to make a call," I interrupted with the quick explanation before I walked to the other side of the room. Ryan's expression suggested he really wanted to ask me what was going on. I ignored it.

At the other wall, my back to the men, I called Catherine. "Do you have a minute?"

She heard the tone in my voice. "What's the matter?"

"Do you know who was killed last night? Or this morning, I suppose," I corrected myself.

"I haven't heard anything," she answered, which was a disappointment. I filled her in on what Orlando the friendly vampire assistant told me, and she said she'd do some digging and call me back as soon as possible. After disconnecting the call, I turned to find myself face to face with Ryan. I must have really been absorbed in my call to miss his approach.

"What murder?" he asked without preamble, his eyes guarded but not unfriendly.

"I don't know yet. Someone with a connection to the set."

"Where's Derek?"

I knew what he was thinking, but I needed to slow him down. "He's gone to check on the crew members connected to the person who was killed. At least that's what I was told," I amended.

"That's an amazing coincidence. Derek being connected to two murders." I heard the accusation in Ryan's tone.

"I agree," I responded slowly, "which is why I called Catherine. To try to gather additional intel."

Ryan smiled at my use of the word intel. Unexpectedly, he reached out to twirl one of my blond curls. "I've missed you."

Hello, left field! "I've missed you too."

"I'm sorry about the other night."

"Me too. I know you want to know more."

"I do. But, I don't want to push you." His hand caressed my cheek and I leaned into it.

We gazed goofily at each other for a moment and then my phone vibrated, breaking the connection. My cheek felt cold when he removed his hand.

"It's Catherine," I told him, receiving the call. He stepped away to provide privacy.

"I have info," she said gleefully. "Although maybe I shouldn't sound so happy. A woman is dead."

"Don't worry about it. What did you find out?"

"The woman who was killed was Sophie Chase, a cinematographer. Beaten to death in her home last night.

No forced entry, though the front door was unlocked. So, she either knew her attacker or at least didn't feel threatened by him or her."

"Probably right, Sherlock," I agreed with a small smile.

I heard Catherine smile through the phone. "She wasn't going to work on *Vampire Nights* because she had another gig lined up in LA, but she was tight with much of your crew. Which is why half of them aren't on set this evening."

"Human or Other?"

"Human, I believe."

"Who found her?"

"A neighbor walking his dog saw her front door open and investigated. Found the body in the front hallway, reportedly covered in blood."

This part of the story bothered Catherine. Even I blanched at the notion of someone being beaten to death. Vampires might have killed for blood in the past. At least the human was bewitched first.

"Any suspects?"

"Ryan's not gonna like this," Catherine warned.

I closed my eyes, foreseeing the answer to my next question. "Why?"

"You can't tell him."

"I won't," though it pained me to make that promise. "Jim Freeman."

I gasped and compulsively looked at Ryan, who returned my look quizzically. I turned away and lowered my voice. "Any other suspects?"

"Nope. My source in the LVMPD says an arrest is imminent."

"He's already on bail," I exclaimed and felt Ryan boring a hole in the back of my head. He had to have heard that. I resolutely did not turn to face him.

"I know. He'll never get bail for this second charge. He's in jail until the trial – or alternate evidence is found."

"Don't remind me."

CHAPTER FOURTEEN

"Catherine confirmed another body has been found and is being investigated as a homicide," I informed Ryan after ending the call.

"And you suspect Jim?"

"He's a likely suspect."

Ryan took the news better than expected. Just a simple question. "What do we do now?"

"I'm guessing filming isn't happening tonight," I explained. "Time for a field trip."

After informing Orlando that we'd be leaving – and he didn't look too surprised – Ryan silently followed me back to my car.

"Where are we going?"

We were zipping along the 215 heading from Summerlin toward Henderson when he asked. I was frankly surprised he waited that long.

"We are heading for the crime scene."

Ryan laughed. "Of course, we are. Are they going to let us in?"

"Leave that to me," I said cryptically with a quick glance at his face. He smiled.

I parked across the street from the house. There was no way we'd miss it since it had yellow crime scene tape across the door. I was preparing to work my vampire voodoo on any officers standing watch, but nobody was there. I felt some disappointment. That must mean they already finished gathering their evidence.

Ryan exited the car with me and followed me to the front door. It was dark. I hoped no spying eyes had seen us. I carefully removed the yellow tape from one side of the door frame. It dangled from the other side, and I found the image forlorn and disturbing. I refocused my attention and tried the door. Naturally, it was locked.

"Now what? Are you going to knock it down?" Ryan said this with a laugh, though I noticed he kept glancing behind us and at the neighbors' houses.

I was in a quandary. I didn't have magical lock picking skills. I did have the strength to simply break the lock. I didn't particularly want to demonstrate this in front of Ryan. Gaining access to the house would not be worth the questions it would bring.

"Time for Plan B," I announced, and strode through the grass. Ryan, startled by my move, hurried to catch up.

We reached the neighbor's house and I knocked on the door before Ryan could ask what I was doing.

An older man holding a leash answered the door and I was confident I guessed correctly.

"Good evening, sir. I'm friends with Sophie Chase from next door and I was wondering if you could answer a few questions."

The man squinted at me. "Are you a reporter?"

"No, sir. A friend. I'm trying to find out what happened." I opened my eyes wide and faked like I was struggling not to cry. I felt like a heel, but it worked.

"I'm Joshua," he said, extending his hand for a handshake. "I'm the one that found her." His face clouded at the memory, less than 24 hours old.

"I can't imagine how hard that must have been," I commiserated.

"She was so young. So friendly. She always had a nice word for Baxter." He held up the leash. "My Basset Hound rescue. I was about to take him for a walk."

"We don't want to hold you up. Do you mind if we walk with you?"

"I don't see why not."

Ryan and I waited at the door while Joshua moved into the house and returned with Baxter on a leash. Joshua locked the door and then the four of us started walking down the street. I could tell Joshua was a bit hesitant yet wanted to help Sophie's friend.

"Would you mind telling us what you told the police officer?"

"I don't see what it can hurt," he agreed. "Baxter and I were returning from our walk late last night. We normally go around this time, but I had been delayed at work, so it was closer to 11 p.m., maybe even closer to midnight. I don't remember exactly."

"That's okay," I assured him.

"I didn't notice anything when I left the house, but when I was returning, I saw that the door was open."

"If I may interrupt, did you not notice anything when you left because everything looked normal, or because you didn't look in that direction?" This distinction was important because it could establish a timeline for events.

"The cops asked the same question and I honestly don't know. I wasn't really paying close attention. I would never have thought it would matter, you know?" He sounded so sad not being certain that I felt bad asking him to relive it.

"That's okay, Joshua. Every little bit helps," I soothed him.

"I approached the open door – and I saw it from the street because light was coming out the door, which doesn't happen if the door is closed," he added. Ryan and I nodded understanding. "I knocked on the door and called out Sophie's name. I didn't receive a reply. I've lived next door to her for years and I've never known her to leave her door open. I had a bad feeling, so I decided to enter."

"Did you consider calling the police?" Ryan asked.

"No," Joshua admitted. "Even though I had a bad feeling, I had nothing really to base it on. And I know how busy Metro is. I figured, this was that one-off where she thought she closed it but she didn't." He shrugged. "When I walked in, she was right there."

I heard him swallow and his heartbeat increased. "She was on the floor. There was blood everywhere. Under her, on her, on the walls. I went to her, to check for a pulse, you know? There wasn't one. She was dead."

We walked several steps in silence before I spoke. "This may be an odd question. Do you remember if her skin felt warm or cold?"

"That's not odd, the police asked the same thing," Joshua responded. "Her neck felt cool. That was part of how I knew she was dead, even as I was checking for breathing and a pulse."

He shuddered, and I touched his hand for support. He looked at me gratefully.

"I have another odd question," Ryan interjected. Joshua looked at him. "What did it smell like?"

"Funny you should ask that. In addition to the smell of the—" he paused, "blood, there was another smell. It smelled like the outdoors."

"What do you mean?" Ryan followed up and I knew the path he was charging down.

"I distinctly remember after calling 9-1-1 and waiting for the police to arrive that I thought I smelled the outdoors. I wondered if Sophie had gotten a new scented candle. She loved those things."

"Could the smell be described as woody?"

"Yeah, I suppose so," Joshua allowed with a slow nod of his head.

I saw the triumphant look on Ryan's face and knew exactly what he was thinking. I focused on Joshua. "Is there anything else you saw, heard…or smelled," I added, "that you think could be useful?"

Joshua thought for a moment. "No, that's everything. That's what I told the police. Well, except for that bit about the smell," he contradicted himself. "They didn't ask."

"That's okay," Ryan assured him. "You can always call them tomorrow to let them know if you think it might be important."

Joshua looked at us for guidance. "Do you think it's important?"

"I'd call," Ryan told him decidedly. "Let the police decide if it's important or not." Joshua nodded.

By now, we had walked the loop of his neighborhood and were approaching my car and Joshua's house. I indicated the Fiat.

"This is us," I explained. "We'll let you get back to your evening." I took one of Joshua's hands in both of mine. "Thank you so much for talking with us."

"You're welcome," he responded. "I'm sorry for your loss."

"Thank you," Ryan and I said in unison. Joshua smiled. Ryan and I exchanged wry glances.

We remained standing next to my car watching Joshua lead Baxter home. Once the older man was safely inside, we entered the vehicle.

"That tells us everything we need to know."

"It does?" I responded cautiously. I had more information than he did.

"Well, yes. Didn't you hear what Joshua said? He smelled that woody smell. The same as Jim reported."

"And from this, you've concluded that Derek is the killer?" I asked the question to buy time. I wouldn't lie to Ryan, but I promised Catherine I wouldn't tell him Jim's arrest was imminent. Heck, it might have even happened.

Ryan gave me a look. "Um, yes. Haven't you?" His eyes narrowed. "Or do you agree with Catherine that Jim is the killer?"

"Wait a minute, Catherine never said that she thinks Jim is the killer," I disagreed.

"I heard you tell her, 'he's already on bail', during your conversation," he countered. "Are you telling me you weren't talking about Jim?"

That I could answer. "You are correct that we were talking about Jim."

Ryan didn't like this non-answer. "But you don't think Derek could be the killer. Is it because of your history with him?"

"Watch your tone," I responded without thinking and felt Ryan's physical reaction to my harsh words. I looked over at him and tried a half-smile. "I agree with you that it is troubling hearing about a woody smell at both murders. But, it doesn't mean it's the *same* woody smell."

Ryan actually rolled his eyes. "Please. Are you kidding? What are the odds that there'd be an unusual woody smell at both murders?"

"I agree it's interesting," I placated. "I'm not saying Derek isn't the killer. I'm not saying he isn't capable of it. I'm just not seeing a motive." I shrugged.

"What is Jim's motive? At least for this murder, since the police already assumed a motive for Monica's murder." The bitterness in his voice was unmistakable.

"I don't know," I admitted.

"Then why would Catherine say Jim is a suspect?"

I didn't answer.

"What else did she tell you?"

I ignored the suspicion in his voice.

He stared out the window, his jaw clenched. Tension rolled off him.

"I know he's your friend," I tried to amend. "I'm not saying he's the killer. I'm trying to maintain an open mind."

Ryan's posture softened. "I know. Thank you. I appreciate that," he acknowledged. "This is so hard. I've known Jim a long time and I know he's not the killer."

Before I could decide how to respond, Ryan's phone rang. "It's Jim!"

Ryan answered, and I heard Jim already talking to someone in the background. My heart sank. I knew what was coming. "Jim? Jim, are you talking to me?"

"Ryan, can you hear me? I've been arrested again."

CHAPTER FIFTEEN

Not eavesdropping was impossible in a car, so I started driving away, making a show of staring straight ahead while Ryan spoke with Jim. Of course, I heard every word on both sides.

"Did you say you've been arrested?"

"Yes."

"Why did you call me? Don't you need your one call for your attorney?"

"Apparently, that's just in the movies. I already spoke to my lawyer and she's told me I won't get bail this time."

"What? Why not?"

"Because I'm already on bail. I'm going to jail."

"Do you know why they arrested you?"

"I haven't been questioned yet. According to my lawyer, the police think I was having an affair with the victim."

"That's crazy. You would never cheat on Monica."

"I know. I don't even know the poor woman who was killed," Jim said, voice hitching on the last word. "I mean, I'd seen her before, but I didn't know her."

Ryan's heart rate jumped, signaling this statement caught him off-guard like it did me.

"You'd seen her? Where?"

"I was introduced to her at the theater. Oh my god," he exhaled loudly. "It was that night. I was introduced to her the night of Monica's mu- death. Do you think that means anything?"

"I don't know," Ryan responded. My mind was racing. It couldn't be unrelated. I didn't believe in coincidences. Certainly not ones looming large like that. Jim, Monica, Sophie, and Derek were all there that night. What did it mean?

"I can't believe they think I killed her," Jim continued, unable to sustain his brief excitement.

"What evidence do they have?"

"I have no idea. Lawyer didn't say."

"Is there anything I can do to help?" Ryan asked.

"Find out who really did it," he answered softly.

"We're working on that."

"You and Evie?"

"Yes," he confirmed. I glanced in his direction in time to see the disappointed look on his face and knew that we were likely going to have a confrontation.

"God, I hope you come up with something," Jim finished, his despair wrenching my gut.

Maybe he wasn't guilty? If he was, he was one heck of an actor. Could it really be Derek? I refocused on the conversation in time to hear them ending the call. I chanced a quick look at Ryan again, saw that look of disappointment, and returned to watching the road. I almost wished he'd be angry.

"You knew." A statement, not a question.

"I did."

"You knew he was going to be arrested and you didn't tell me."

I reached my hand toward his, and replaced it on the steering wheel before giving him the opportunity to withdraw. I glanced back and forth between him and the road while we talked.

"I didn't want to put you in an awkward position."

"Why would it?"

"If you knew he was going to be arrested, wouldn't you want to warn him?"

No response.

"I'm sorry it worked out like this. I try to respect and help my friends when I can, just like you're trying to do."

He stared at me a beat.

"I promised Catherine I wouldn't tell you."

"Catherine knew too." Again, a statement not a question.

"She told me in the earlier phone call," I admitted.

Ryan faced forward and closed his eyes. I heard him trying to manage his heartbeat, trying to maintain control.

"Ryan, please understand."

"Understand what? That you're willing to throw my friend under the bus for your ex."

I recoiled as if slapped. "That's not what's going on. You know that. We just talked about it," I said, a touch of exasperation in my voice. It did not go unnoticed.

"Gee, is my being upset bothering you?"

"There's no need for sarcasm," I retorted. "We both want the same thing. The real killer found."

"And you believe it's Jim."

"I believe it's a possibility, yes," I answered. "We're talking in circles here, which is entirely unproductive. Do you still want my help?"

A long silence followed.

I waited for him to decide. The wait was excruciating.

"Yes," he finally answered quietly. "I do." He gave me his adorable lopsided grin.

My relief was palpable. I ignored the feeling and what it might mean. We didn't have time for that. We were trying to catch a killer.

"We were just given a big piece of information," I said, clapping my hands, which seemed only slightly out of place, given the circumstances.

*****

"There's no way I'm letting you put yourself in harm's way."

I arched an eyebrow. "You're not letting me?"

"You know what I mean."

I smiled because, of course, I knew what he meant. It was fun to watch him squirm. We sat on his living room couch, discussing my idea. Which he clearly didn't like.

"At least let me come with you," he insisted.

"No," I answered and watched his jaw tighten.

"Why not?"

"If Derek sees you, then he'll know something's up," I explained again.

"Not if I stay out of sight," he countered.

I sighed. "We're going in circles. We need to either confirm or eliminate Derek as a suspect and the best way to do that is for me to play on his intention to win me back by," I involuntarily shuddered here, "flirting with him to get him to talk. It's a classic."

This time it was Ryan who arched an eyebrow. "Exactly."

"I don't want you to see that."

We stared at each other. His heartbeat increased and his eyes dilated. Now wasn't the time to deal with our mutual attraction. I broke eye contact as he spoke.

"I wouldn't want to see that either, but…"

"We need our best shot at getting him to confess."

"And that's why I want to be there. If he confesses to murder, you could be in harm's way."

There was no way for me to explain that Derek couldn't hurt me – not that he wouldn't, I silently agreed with Ryan – but as a vampire, he had to have permission from our vampire Family to do so. And he didn't have that. I didn't think he did anyway.

"He's not going to hurt me," was all I said.

"I don't understand how you can be so sure," Ryan argued stubbornly.

"I just am. More importantly," I stressed, "if he sees you, all bets are off. You know that."

"Okay, okay. I hear the exasperation in your voice," he acknowledged with a smile. "I'll let you do it your way. I mean, let's do it your way," he corrected himself and we both laughed, though I was mildly surprised he was finally giving in. Alpha men rarely did so. It was a good thing. The real reason I didn't want him there was that I didn't want him to find out Derek and I were vampires. I wasn't ready to have the conversation yet, if I ever was.

"I have one condition."

"Oh really?"

Ryan cupped my chin for a moment with gentle fingers, brushing his thumb along my jaw. "Yes. I want full contact info for Derek, just in case. If you don't check in at a designated time, I want to be able to either contact you myself or provide the information to the authorities." His jugular vein throbbed in his neck and I knew how worried he was for me. I placed one hand on his knee, heard his heartbeat accelerate further in reaction.

"Okay," I agreed. "That sounds reasonable."

Ryan placed his hand over mine. "I wouldn't want anything to happen to you."

"I wouldn't want anything to happen to me, either," I quipped. Ryan squeezed my hand slightly and released.

"What next?"

"Let me text Derek." I scrolled through my contacts until I found him.

I assume filming is going to resume? I'd like to discuss my character. Are you free tonight?

Ryan and I watched my phone, waiting for the response, which seemed to take forever, but really was probably less than a minute.

Great! Meet at my hotel?

Ryan frowned and I shook my head at him. "Wait."

Hotel lounge? Or bar?

LOL, sure.

"Such a punk."

"I don't disagree," I responded.

Where?

Ryan and I waited again and Chandelier Bar popped up. Ryan nodded that he saw.

Got it. See you at midnight?

Yep.

"There. We're set," I needlessly stated. I forwarded Derek's number to Ryan. He nodded when the text arrived.

"Promise you'll call as soon as you're finished?"

"I promise."

"If I don't hear from you by one, I'm calling. And if I can't reach you, I'm calling the authorities," he warned. I was touched by his needless concern.

"I'll be fine. Maybe give me until 1:30. In case it takes longer."

His eyes darkened and I didn't need vampire senses to know what he was imagining.

"I'm not going to sleep with him," I assured him, making a face of disgust.

"Things don't always go the way we plan," he responded.

My eyes widened in surprise. "Do you think I'd sleep with him?"

He didn't answer and my heart sank.

I placed a hand under his chin, lifted his eyes toward mine. "It'll never happen," I assured him.

I was acutely aware of the increase in his physical response to me.

Ryan leaned forward as if to kiss me, and then he pulled back. "Good."

CHAPTER SIXTEEN

Although I grumbled at having to pay for parking on The Strip (really, Las Vegas?), I was glad that Derek at least had the sense to stay at the Cosmopolitan, where the first floor of the Chandelier lounge had the best chocolate martinis ever. Not that I drank them, of course, but they smelled heavenly.

The mass of humanity swarming around me as I approached bombarded me with their physical reactions to the scene. When I was a younger vampire, this would have overwhelmed me; luckily, over time, I'd learned the ability to block or at least filter out some of that noise. The hundreds of beaded chandelier strings around the lounge sparkled and reflected the light – almost everywhere. I zeroed in on a dead spot near the bar. Derek. He absorbed the light and energy around him like a, well, vampire. I shook my head at my own silliness.

He sensed me when I ascended the few lighted steps and turned left to the nearest circular couch. He was seated alone, his energy keeping the humans away. Even while I watched, a drunk couple approached, started to enter the enclosed area, and abruptly veered off. I chuckled. It was a good location, facing the bar, our backs to the room. We'd pitch our voices below human perception and use Derek's glamour to mask sounds, but it was still best to take precautions. Some people had been known to read lips and I had a vampire friend called out that way once. Awkward.

Derek was as spectacular as ever, his tall frame folded into the seat, one foot resting on the knee of his other leg. Tonight, he wore all black: tight black jeans, gleaming black leather boots, fitted black button-down shirt with the first three buttons again undone. Had this become his signature style? His dark eyes followed me while I walked toward him and entered the seating area. His skin practically glowed in the mood lighting. He smirked when I carefully sat several feet from him. He smelled like the woods.

"Good evening, Evie. You look like candy," he said, his eyes sliding up and down my figure. "Good enough to eat." I was glad I didn't bother to change into something more seductive from my daisy blouse and yellow pants I wore to set earlier in the evening. I squirmed under his gaze and needlessly adjusted my beret. His smile widened.

Thank goodness, he'd mistaken my reaction as a positive, when really, I wanted to hurl.

"Hi, Derek," I responded, trying a smile, hoping it wasn't as fake as it felt. "You look…nice." I faltered. I noticed that he ordered a chocolate martini for me to pretend to drink and I picked it up, inhaling deeply. I set the drink back on the table and raised my eyes to his.

We stared at each other, neither able to read the other. Derek slowly smiled. "You called this meeting," he reminded me.

"Right," I agreed. "I wanted to discuss filming. I assume the shoot is still happening."

"Yes."

"Do you have any idea when that might be?"

"No."

"Any changes to the cast and crew?"

"No."

Ugh, this was going nowhere fast. His monosyllabic answers allowed for zero chance at expansion. I frowned.

"Isn't this what you wanted?"

"I don't follow."

"You just frowned. But, isn't this what you wanted? To talk about filming," he elaborated.

"I – well, yes."

"No, it isn't."

"It isn't?"

"No."

"Now I'm confused," I admitted, not following his train of thought.

Derek scooted closer. I stiffened. He laughed low and sexy. "You know that's not why you wanted to meet."

"It's not?"

"No."

"Then why did I want to meet?" He surely didn't know I suspected him of murder.

"I saw your reaction when I told you I wanted you back."

My revulsion? I stayed silent.

"You want me back, too," he explained.

Ah, narcissism. There you were. I shook my head in a non-response.

"It's okay. I know this was unexpected."

"Yes?" I asked this, unsure what response he expected.

Derek reached for my hand and I allowed him to hold it. He stroked my palm. One hundred years ago, this might have worked. Tonight, not so much. At least I had my opening.

"I don't know what I want," I admitted, honestly. Not him, of course. But, Ryan? That was another story.

"We can take it slow," he whispered, sidling even closer so that I could feel the chill coming off him. He placed his other hand on my knee, rubbing lightly. I forced myself not to withdraw and smiled instead. "I've changed, Evie. I can be the man you need me to be. The man you fell in love with. The man I was before you married me. In the beginning."

"Reset to one?" I asked sadly, as if that were even possible after everything we'd been through.

Derek laughed at my movie production humor. "Exactly. Reset to one – go back to the beginning."

"I'm worried about everything going on," I said, to try for a redirect. His hands stopped their movement but remained in position.

"What are you worried about, kitten?"

That I reacted to. He hadn't called me by his nickname for me in decades. I smiled quickly to cover my discomfort and glanced away. A tall guy walking past our couch glanced briefly at me. Something about him seemed familiar. Who could tell with his backwards baseball cap and sunglasses? Inside. How pretentious. I refocused on Derek.

"I'm worried about the murders."

Derek's fingers tightened on my knee before releasing. I saw the tension in his face but his response was light.

"Murders? What are you talking about?"

I pulled away completely from him with the question, aghast, and only partly pretending. "What do you mean, what murders am I talking about?"

Derek shrugged. "I know a friend of the crew was killed. Was there another murder?"

I eyed him carefully. This could be a moment of truth. "Monica? Monica Freeman? We talked about her murder," I reminded him pointedly.

"Oh, that," he replied with a dismissive wave. "Wasn't her husband arrested for that?"

"Yes."

"And wasn't he implicated in the other murder?"

"Yes."

"Then why would you be worried? They have the killer in custody."

"If he's the killer."

Derek eyed me for a beat. "What makes you think he's not the killer?"

I picked up the chocolate martini again to think for a second before responding. "I think it's a little too convenient," I answered slowly.

"Maybe that's just because he's guilty," Derek countered with a shrug.

I lifted the drink to my nose again and inhaled. Dang, that was good. I set it down and stared at my ex-husband. Here we go.

"Witnesses at the scenes of both murders reported smelling a woody scent." Derek started at this comment but said nothing. "And Jim isn't the only person with connections to both victims."

CHAPTER SEVENTEEN

"Jim? I didn't realize you knew the accused or the victims." Derek's eyes glittered.

"I don't. Not really."

"Then why do you care?"

"I just do," I said, not wanting to elaborate.

Derek's eyes hardened. "It's that other guy."

My eyes widened, theatrically I imagined. "Whatever do you mean?"

"Cut the nonsense, Evie," he snorted. "I knew there was something going on between you and that actor," he spat out the last word.

"This has nothing to do with Ryan," I argued.

"Ryan? I thought you said at the audition that you just met him." He glared at me.

"What are you accusing me of? I think you're deflecting."

"From what?"

"I saw your reaction when I mentioned the scent the witnesses reported. A scent described very much like what you smell like tonight."

Derek shifted slightly, his only indication that I hit a nerve. "Lots of cologne and aftershave smell like the woods. It's manly," he explained.

"I'm not an idiot. I'm aware of that. I just find it highly coincidental."

"Why do you care?" He asked again, this time lifting both hands at me in a clear gesture of irritation.

I glanced around to see if anybody was paying attention to his raised voice, before remembering the glamour. I noticed the pretentious guy from earlier sitting at the bar. His sunglasses reflected in the mirror.

"I care because I like humanity and I don't want to see an innocent man go to prison."

"You think I'm the killer? Because of some odor?"

"Yes, I do." This might not be 100% true, but I was leaning more and more in that direction.

Derek broke eye contact and sighed heavily. "Dang, Evie, a guy can't catch a break."

"What do you mean?"

"I did it. You're right. I killed both of the women." He watched me carefully to gauge my reaction.

"I don't know what to say." This was the truth. I was stunned. I waited for him to elaborate.

"The whole thing was a mistake."

"A mistake?"

He shook his head.

"How do you mistakenly kill not one, but two, people?"

Derek had the good grace to at least glance away, seemingly embarrassed.

Although, since I knew he didn't care one whit about humanity, there must be another reason. I decided to wait him out. I picked up my chocolate martini and pretended to sip it, inhaling the amazing aroma.

A sigh captured my attention.

I peered over the top of the drink at my ex-husband.

"It was just a job," he finally stated.

"A job? What kind of job requires you to—" I stopped with the sudden realization. "Oh."

Derek nodded. "I'm a Cleaner."

He said nothing more. He didn't need to. Like organized crime, vampire families had Cleaners who took care of issues before they became bigger issues.

"You were sent to Vegas to clean someone?" I asked the question slowly, trying to wrap my mind around the fact that Derek was a Cleaner. When did that happen?

As if hearing my unasked question, Derek elaborated. "A few decades ago, I was bored and looking for something new to do. I put out feelers, wanting to do more for the Family, and this was what popped up."

My mouth fell open. "You've been killing humans for decades?" I genuinely didn't know what else to say.

Derek rolled his eyes. "You always have cared too much for the vermin. Do you even like being a vampire?"

I balled my fists, wanting nothing more than to knock that smug look off his face. He grinned, seeing my reaction, and knowing I wouldn't draw that kind of attention to us. And, dammit, he was right. I released my fists and rested my hands lightly on my knees, thinking.

"The first woman was an accident," he continued as if telling a fun fact. "I was given information that the target would be at the theater that night. It was last minute information and it was wrong." He shrugged, clearly not caring that he killed the wrong person.

"Monica was a case of mistaken identity?"

"Yes, Evie, good grief, are you being deliberately slow?"

"No. I'm not being deliberately slow," I responded between clenched teeth. "I'm trying to understand what a colossal moron you are." That hit home and anger radiated off of Derek in response.

"So, after you messed up…" I prompted.

He might have wanted to respond to my insult. Instead he chose to continue the story.

"I framed the husband. When that didn't seem to be sufficient, I killed that other woman to cement the frame job."

I tilted my head, wondering how I ever could have loved the man before me, even before he was a vampire. This had to have been there all along. I glared at him. "You ruined three lives and – oh my goodness – there's still a woman out there in danger!" The realization slammed into me like the proverbial ton of bricks. "You can't kill anybody else," I warned.

Derek laughed. "I'm not going to," he assured me.

This stopped me cold. "You're not? What about the original contract?"

He glanced away again. "Yeah, so it turned out she was never in Las Vegas at all. She was in Las Cruces. New Mexico," he elaborated. "Before you worry about trying to warn her, she apparently got wind of the hit, and has gone underground, so for now, the contract has been pulled." He smiled widely. "See. It's all finished." He moved in closer and placed his hand on my knee again. "We can forget all about this unpleasantness and focus on the movie. And us."

Before I could respond, I sensed motion as someone approached. Derek and I both turned towards the person, frowning because no human should be comfortable in our energy dead zone.

Oh no. Up close, I realized that I recognized the pretentious guy in the backwards ball cap and sunglasses.

Ryan. He whipped the sunglasses off of his face. Boy did he look pissed!

Derek chuckled and didn't move. I stood immediately, put my hands on Ryan's chest. He jerked away like he'd been burned. My hands fell to my sides. I didn't know what to do.

"How could you?" Ryan hissed this at me.

Wait? Me? "What did I do?" I asked in confusion.

"You blamed Jim for the murders. You tried to convince me he could be a killer. And the entire time you were protecting your ex-husband. Who you're clearly fonder of than you let on," Ryan finished with a snarl.

How was I going to fix this? Before I could respond, Ryan continued, turning on Derek.

"You. You killed my friend Monica and some other innocent woman, then framed Jim for both."

"Thanks for the recap, sport," Derek said indolently.

Ryan raised his hand to punch Derek and time slowed then stopped. I stared at Ryan frozen in time.

CHAPTER EIGHTEEN

I turned to Derek.

"What are you doing?"

"I'm not about to let that idiot hit me," he explained and stood. "I'm leaving. You can sort this crazy out." Derek rolled his eyes again – had he always been this juvenile, I absently wondered.

"You can't just leave," I countered. "It'll look like you vanished."

"So?"

"We already don't know what Ryan somehow overheard. Which he shouldn't have been able to."

"Who cares?" Derek set his drink down on the table. "I'm leaving," he repeated.

"No."

"No?" An eyebrow lifted at my tone. "Who's going to stop me? You?" He laughed.

"No," I snapped at him. "You're going to choose to stay." I smiled. His own smile faltered.

"Why would I do that?"

"So we can find out what he knows and handle this."

Derek stared hard at me for a moment and then fake sighed. "Fine."

"Return time to its normal speed. Please," I added sweetly.

Derek stepped slightly to the side as time returned to normal. Ryan's punch missed Derek's face completely. Ryan appeared confused both by the fact that he missed and that somehow Derek was now standing.

Ryan's gaze swung between me and Derek, his frown deepening. "What—" he started to say and then stopped.

"Ryan, it's not what you think."

"You weren't flirting with your ex-husband, the killer?"

"This is why I didn't want you to come, remember?" I reminded him in a low voice.

"So I wouldn't see you flirting," he sputtered. "With a killer!"

"Shh," I responded, emphasizing with my hands that we needed him to be quiet.

Ryan opened his mouth to continue, and then didn't. The disappointment on his face wounded me.

"I told you that I might have to," I paused, "flirt with my ex."

"This whole thing was a setup," Derek jumped in, incredulous. I was unclear if he was shocked I didn't want to get back with him or that I would, in his eyes, stoop so low as to set him up.

"Yes, murderer," Ryan growled.

Derek's eyes narrowed to murderous slits. "Shut up, human."

"Oh," as if suddenly remembering, "that's the other thing. You're both clearly delusional. Vampires!" Ryan barked out a laugh.

I looked around, worried someone would hear him, and that reminded me. "How could you hear us?"

Ryan looked at me like I'd grown a second head. "Why does that matter?"

I hesitated. Might as well go all in. "As a human, you should not have been able to hear us talking, if we didn't want you to. We definitely didn't want anybody to."

Ryan unexpectedly looked thoughtful. "Actually, I didn't hear you," he began.

"How did you know what we were saying?"

"I read your lips."

My eyes moved to the mirror over the bar. "In the bar mirror? You read our lips in the mirror?" In spite of myself, I was impressed. Even though a friend got busted in a similar way, it honestly never occurred to me that anybody could read our lips in a mirror. Wouldn't it be backward?

I realized belatedly that Ryan and Derek were staring at me while my mind wandered. "Sorry."

"It doesn't matter. I'm going to the police."

"Who will believe you?" Derek challenged.

"Not that the two of you have delusions of being vampires," Ryan clarified. "It's quite simple. I'll point the police toward you, Derek, by mentioning an overheard conversation, woody smells at both crime scenes, and Evie as a corroborating witness."

His shoulders sagged, maybe not as confident and pleased as the words implied.

I reached out again, placing my hand on his arm. He didn't pull away this time, just gazed at me sadly.

"Please don't," I begged.

"Why not?" he asked hollowly. "It's the truth."

"Yes, it is," I agreed. "But…it puts everybody in danger," I finished vaguely.

"Danger?"

With a sigh, I explained. "If you say anything, it will put you in danger. It will also threaten us with exposure."

"Exposure as what? Crazy people?"

I flinched at his words and his self-satisfied expression dropped a notch.

"We're not crazy. I'm trying to protect us. All of us," I hastened to add.

"No, you're not," he disagreed. "You're threatening me." His small voice broke my heart. I hadn't yet figured out if he and I might have a chance at something, but I felt it being snatched away.

"I'm not." I squeezed Ryan's arms gently and he broke eye contact.

"I am." Derek chose that moment to add his two cents. He smiled wolfishly at Ryan, who pulled completely away from me.

"Derek, good luck with that. Evie," his voice hiccupped. "Good luck with everything."

Ryan and I stared at each other; if I could cry, I think I would have. Derek stewed beside me. With a final half-shrug, Ryan walked away. Away from me. Away from us. Or at least the chance of us.

Derek broke my train of thoughts. "I'm going to kill him. You know that."

"That isn't necessary," I insisted.

"Yes, it is. Plus, I plan to enjoy it." Derek allowed his fangs to descend slightly to emphasize his point. I wanted to throttle him.

"What about a mind wipe?" I offered this alternative frantically. I needed to convince Derek before he left, or Ryan was a dead man.

"No."

"Just no? Why not?"

"How can you love a human who is endangering us?" Derek sounded exasperated but my mind buzzed.

"Love? Who said anything about love?"

"Love, like, lust, whatever. You know what I mean."

"I don't want any more innocents hurt," I maintained. Derek saw through me.

"He's a threat. He knows about us, thus he's endangering us," he repeated slowly like I was a child.

Now I was pissed. "He's not the one endangering us. You are!"

Surprised, Derek laughed. "What are you talking about?"

"Are you kidding? It's bad enough you apparently kill humans regularly. This time, you've killed the wrong people. You don't think that endangers us? Hello?"

Derek didn't miss the sniping tone of my statement and actually looked abashed. "We've buried…mistakes… before," he offered.

I stepped closer to him and stood on my tiptoes to bring my face as close as possible. He looked decidedly uncomfortable.

"This is finished. We are finished. There is no us. I will never take you back, under any circumstances. And if anything happens to Ryan, I'll go to the Family and tell them all about your…mistake," I hissed out the last word, spun on my heels before he could respond, and strode from him, down the short stairs, and through the casino. The noise of people laughing, machines clanging, and music playing swirled around me and in my head while I walked. What did I do now?

CHAPTER NINETEEN

The dark house mocked my intent. Yes, it was 3 in the morning, but since it hadn't been that long since Ryan stormed from the casino floor, I doubted he was actually asleep. I knocked again, deliberately not banging. One, because he had neighbors. And, two, because I didn't want to spook him.

I sighed. He thought I was delusional. He was never going to answer the door. I pulled my phone from my purse to text him. A long shot that he'd respond. I figured it was worth the effort.

Ryan. You know I'm at the door. Please open up.

Nothing. I waited, not patiently. Still nothing.

Ryan. Please let me explain. It's not what you think.

Well, in all honesty, it at least somewhat was, I supposed. I confirmed my ex-husband was a killer. No response from Ryan. Okay, time to pull out all the stops.

Ryan. I'll start knocking on your neighbors' doors and tell them all that I'm worried about you if you don't open the door.

I silently counted to thirty, unsure if I even meant my threat. Probably not. I'd probably just go away—

The door opened and Ryan stood in the opening. His hooded hazel eyes betrayed no sense of his emotions. I tried for a smile. It faltered on my lips. *A mind wipe would be so easy* flashed quickly and I banished the thought immediately. I realized that was my suggestion earlier to Derek, but that was born of desperation. Away from Derek, I was convinced that I could explain this rationally to Ryan. He would understand.

We stared at each other. My eyes drank in his mussed auburn hair, cut short yet still long enough to run my fingers through. A forest green t-shirt stretched across his broad shoulders, inviting my eyes to travel the length of him. He didn't miss this and, despite himself, I was guessing, his eyes darkened with desire.

Abruptly, he turned, breaking eye contact, and retreated into the interior of his house. I took the door left open as an invitation and followed. His comfortable blue corduroy couch threatened to swallow even his tall frame. I perched on the edge, next to him but not touching. He leaned forward, head in his hands.

"Ryan," I ventured, just as he spoke.

"Evie."

"You go first."

"No, you," he insisted.

"Okay." Now I was silent, formulating what I wanted to say in such a way that I didn't sound even more bat-shit crazy than he already thought I was.

"I'm sorry." I paused, knowing this was completely inadequate, and yet, unsure exactly what I was apologizing *for*.

Ryan must have sensed this because he lifted his head, eyes narrowed. "How could you?"

"How could I what?"

"I'm such a fool." He looked away.

Tentatively, I placed a hand on his knee. He jerked away from me like I did earlier this evening with Derek. Rejection hurt. I placed my hands in my lap, silently imploring him to look at me again. Amazingly he did. The hurt there was like a knife to my heart.

"You used me."

"What are you talking about?"

Ryan stood and paced the small room. "I should have known something was up when you were so quick to blame Jim."

"The police arrested him," I pointed out.

He stopped moving. "I knew he was innocent. You insisted he was guilty."

Anger rose in me. "Wait a minute. I never insisted he was guilty."

"You sure seemed certain of yourself."

"People are usually who they appear to be," I snapped.

"Yes. They. Are."

We glared at each other for a few long seconds before speaking. "I admit I was wrong," I allowed. "But why are you so mad at me?" I was genuinely perplexed by the strength of his reaction, and my own anger drained away.

His heartbeat increased. "Why? You don't understand why?"

"No," I whispered. "Please, tell me."

At my whisper, his expression softened. "You were working both sides, making me believe that you and I…" The naked fear in his eyes at this unfinished statement startled me and I looked away. "That you were interested in finding out the truth," he adjusted his comment.

"I was. I am," I insisted, standing to approach him. His expression hardened again and I stopped short of reaching out. "I wasn't working both sides. I don't even like my ex-husband," I finished, the revulsion so strong in my voice that I couldn't believe Ryan didn't hear it.

Ryan closed his eyes and breathed deeply. "I don't know." His eyes reopened and I saw sadness there. "It's too convenient. You point the finger at Jim. Derek just happens to come to town. We go to his audition to gather information. Then, you insist you need to cozy up to him to get the truth."

Anger flared bright and painful again. "I did not *insist* I needed to cozy up to him. I told you that was the best way of getting the information from him. And it was. It *worked.* We got his confession. And, dammit, you agreed to the plan."

Ryan fidgeted, maybe unsure what to do with my comments. "I did. Because I didn't understand what was really at play."

"What are you talking about?" I was embarrassed to realize I yelled this and stopped to focus my thoughts before speaking again. "There was nothing else at play besides finding out what really happened to Monica and Sophie. That was all."

"Let's say for argument's sake that I believe you."

Hope filled me and I searched his face for understanding.

"What about the other nonsense?"

I opened my mouth and nothing came out. You would think after nearly 100 years, I would be more adept at handling humans when they found out I was a vampire. Of course, I was usually much better at hiding it.

"Nothing to say," he taunted.

"I don't know what to say," I admitted and his smirk disappeared, his shoulders slumping.

"Do you really believe that you're vampires? Why would you make something like that up? The only reason I can think of is to try to freak me out, to keep me from going to the police about your ex-husband. And that brings me back to why I would believe you were working both sides, and really don't want to turn him in." Ryan said this in a rush, and my mouth fell open in shock. No wonder he was mad at me.

I opened and closed my mouth several times, trying to find the right words to explain. To make him believe. He crossed his arms over his chest, putting his wall even higher. Nevertheless, I reached out again and placed my fingertips on his forearm. He didn't pull away, but the muscle underneath tightened in response.

"Ryan. It genuinely is not like that. You are correct that I don't want you to go to the police." I articulated, choosing my words oh so carefully. His lips thinned with his displeasure at my words.

"Not for the reason that you think." I closed my eyes briefly and then stared directly into his. "You must hear me. I know it sounds crazy. I wouldn't believe it if I wasn't one. Derek and I *are* vampires."

He turned away with an eye roll and shake of his head, knocking my hands off. I reached back out, stopped a hair's breadth from his shoulder before dropping my hand back to my side. "If you go to the police, I don't know what he might do. It's better if you let my people handle it."

Ryan laughed then. I heard the undercurrent of anger and hysteria, knew this was not a happy laugh. He faced me again. "Your people?" he asked, quirking an eyebrow. "You should leave." He sounded so resigned that I wanted to engulf him in a hug, comfort him while he tried to process this information turning his world upside down.

I didn't. I knew it was unwanted. "Okay," was all I said.

"I don't think it's a good idea for you to reach out to me again."

I nodded, in understanding if not agreement. "Goodbye, Ryan," I whispered as I turned from him. I trudged to the front door. Hoping he'd call out. Knowing he wouldn't. Resisting my own urge to turn to look at him one last time.

Exiting the house, I pulled the door closed behind me. I walked to my car, sat inside, turned the key. I drove without awareness back to my condo. My deadened heart felt even more hollow.

CHAPTER TWENTY

"Evelyn?"

"Good grief, Robin! You surely know it's not a good idea to sneak up on a vampire, right?" I asked the talent agent who materialized out of a dark corner of the parking garage when I exited my car.

"You were seen again with Derek at the Cosmopolitan and the councilwoman would like an update on his role," Robin Landon spoke like I'd said nothing.

Swallowing my irritation, I stared at the insipid face of the minion. "Do you guys have nothing better to do than track our movements?"

Robin did not respond; she simply waited.

I sighed. Might as well get it over with. "Yes, Derek and I met at the Cosmopolitan. Did you know they have amazing chocolate martinis at the Chandelier Bar?"

Her eyebrows furrowed in confusion. "You don't drink."

"No, I don't." I left her actual question unanswered.

"And?"

"Oh, fine. I imagine somebody else could provide the information too," I finally allowed. "Derek killed Monica Freeman on accident – mistaken identity – and then killed Sophie Chase in an ill-thought-out plan to hide the first murder."

Robin's eyebrows furrowed again.

"You're not immortal. Keep doing that and you'll get wrinkles," I offered.

"That's it?"

"Man, you're no fun," I told the woman. "There was an actual hit ordered, but that person has gone underground."

Robin sighed. Out of irritation or in response to my information, I couldn't tell. "Anything else?"

"Nope," I responded cheerfully. "And, please pass along a message to your boss. The next time the councilwoman has a question for me, she can ask me herself. I'm not interested in continuing to parlay with lackeys," I stated pointedly. I strode away from Robin but didn't miss her ears redden at the insult.

Probably not a good idea to push the demon. Whatever.

****

When I awoke from my slumber the next evening as the sun was setting, a glance at my phone informed me that the past day was quite exciting. Notifications of a series of increasingly frantic texts from Catherine filled my phone's screen.

I know you're sleeping. Call me when you get up.

The you-know-what is about to hit the fan; call me.

The sun is setting; are you up yet?? Call me!!

Evie! I have news about Ryan and your ex.

That last text, in particular, worried me. I had already been uncertain about whether or not Derek would stay away from Ryan. I mean, Derek clearly understood my threat to report him to the Family if he harmed Ryan. But this was Derek. His ability to think ahead was directly proportional to his ego's belief that he could get away with anything.

With a groan of frustration, I called Catherine. She answered on the first ring.

"Evie, thank goodness you called!"

"What's going on with Ryan and Derek?"

"Did you know Ryan reported Derek to the police? Said he's the killer?"

I was silent for a beat while I processed the information. I had truly hoped Ryan would not do this. Of course, I never pushed the issue last night.

"You knew!" Catherine answered her own question.

"I had hoped he wouldn't," I explained, my mind racing.

"What does this mean? Did you guys find proof that Derek did it? What will happen next? I mean, they can't really incarcerate a vampire. Right?"

I chuckled at Catherine's rapid-fire questions in conversation with herself. "Take a breath, Catherine."

A giggle came across the line in response. "Sorry. You know how excitable I am."

"No different than me," I assured her with a commiserating eye roll. I quickly brought Catherine up to speed with the events of last night.

Between me and Derek. Between me, Derek, and Ryan. And, finally, between me and Ryan. Oh, yeah, and between me and Robin in the parking garage.

"Wow, you had a busy night," she said, in the ultimate understatement.

"How do you know Ryan reported Derek for the murders?"

"Oh, right. After the second murder involved the entertainment industry, I asked a friend with Metro to keep me updated. My source called this afternoon to give me a heads up that an actor had come in and pointed the finger at a producer in town doing a movie. Even before he gave me the names, I figured it was Ryan and Derek."

"Clearly," I agreed. "Did your source say anything else?"

"Oh yeah. They're looking to bring Derek in as a *person of interest* in the murders."

"We both know what that means."

"They think he's their best suspect. Confidentially, my source said they never really thought Jim was the killer, especially when the second one seemed so flimsy."

"Why did they arrest him then?"

"District attorney who has sights on the mayor's office. Maybe even the governor."

"Does the politicking ever end?"

"I don't even need to answer that."

"No, you don't." I paused to think. "As far as you know, though, Metro hasn't arrested Derek yet?"

"I haven't gotten another call, no."

"Ryan really should have let me handle this," I groused. "Now the idiot has gone and put himself directly in Derek's crosshairs."

"You're pretty sure he'll kill him?"

"For implicating him in murder? Absolutely. I was fairly confident I convinced Derek not to harm Ryan, and to let me handle it. But, now? I'd say all bets are off at this point. My only hope is that I have time since Derek just woke up too."

"Then I'd better let you go. Save the man in distress."

I heard the smile in her voice, knew she was joking to lighten the mood.

"Thanks. Call me if you hear anything else."

"Of course. Good luck."

We disconnected and I sat for a moment in bed clutching my phone. Hoping against hope, I called Ryan.

"You have reached the voicemail of Ryan Walter. Sorry I missed your call. Please leave a message and I'll get back to you as soon as possible."

I ended the call and stared blankly ahead.

If you're not dead already.

CHAPTER TWENTY-ONE

Uh-oh. I parked my car behind Derek's black Porsche 911 and flew up the walkway to Ryan's house. My heightened hearing already knew they were fighting. They were also still talking, so that was a good sign. Mostly.

I barged in the front door. Both men's heads swiveled to me, registered who I was, and then swung back toward each other. They were clearly invested in this fight. Derek stood stock still about half a foot from Ryan, who had grabbed ahold of Derek's shoulders. Interestingly, Derek didn't appear to be physically fighting back. This was good, since with his vampire strength, Ryan didn't stand a chance. But, it was disconcerting. The smirk on his face though was exactly what I expected.

"Why are you even here? I didn't invite you in," Ryan taunted. I rolled my eyes at the attempted vampire insult. Even though Ryan didn't believe we were really vampires, he apparently knew the mythology. Although it wasn't true. We could go anywhere we wanted. Humans didn't have to invite us in.

"A little birdy told me that you went to the police," Derek slowly spoke. His eyes flicked to me and then back. "I thought we had an understanding."

"An understanding? You're a killer! I made it very clear I would go to the police." He abruptly released Derek, who smoothed down his rumpled shirt.

Derek turned to me then. "Actually, I thought *you* said this was handled."

I shrugged. "What can I say? I learned about it at the same time you did."

Derek and I simultaneously turned to face Ryan, who wore such an expression of disgust that I wanted to cry.

Ryan and I made eye contact and I saw sadness warring with the disgust, and this heartened me. Maybe we could still fix us. This. I mean, this.

"Gentlemen," I urged them calmly. "Let's talk this through. There has to be a satisfactory solution."

Derek snorted. Really. "Kitten, you know the only solution is this human's death."

Ryan and I talked over each other.

"Dang it, Derek, don't call me kitten!"

"Did you just threaten me?"

Ryan took a step toward Derek, who flexed his muscles. Vampires took peacocking to new heights.

I stepped between the two men. "Seriously, nobody has to die." I shot daggers at Derek. "There is a solution."

Derek remained silent. Ryan grudgingly asked, "What is the solution?"

"Ryan, you and I want Jim out of jail, right?" He nodded.

"Derek, you and I want to keep vampire society out of the spotlight, right?" A very pregnant pause before he nodded.

"Then the answer is to give the police an iron-clad killer," I finished triumphantly.

Ryan sneered. "Your answer is to frame someone else? We have the killer right here. He admitted it." This last said almost desperately, trying to convince me.

Derek shook his head dismissively. "Nice try, Evie. No. The answer is to kill this human."

I turned to face the true threat and squared off with Derek. We were both vampires; he knew besting me was not a forgone conclusion, like it would be with Ryan. "You'll have to go through me first." My voice was deadly quiet. Ryan's breathing and heart rate quickened.

"No, Evie." Ryan sounded worried and that made me happy, for some odd reason.

With the element of surprise, and seeing my split-second distraction, Derek struck. He pushed me sideways, where I fell rather unceremoniously to the carpet. Boring brown, but rather plush, I thought distractedly.

By the time I rose to my feet, Derek had grabbed Ryan around the throat and begun squeezing. Ryan fought the best he could. He was zero match for the killer vampire. Ryan kicked his legs out, aiming for Derek's crotch. Hit, Derek winced. That was it.

Ryan's hands grasped at Derek's, trying unsuccessfully to wrench them free from his neck. Ryan was turning an unhealthy shade of purple. I jumped into the fray with a sigh.

Derek released Ryan's neck after I kicked his knees out from under him from behind. Ryan coughed violently, filling his lungs with air, and I was pleased to see his face was pinking back up nicely. Derek had already recovered from my hit and grabbed me in a bear hug, his mouth an inch from my ear.

Despite the action, he remained bloodless and cold, cool air from his words tingling my earlobe.

"I don't want to hurt you, too."

"You won't get the chance," I whispered as I launched us, still in an embrace, back toward the living room wall. The plaster cracked where we hit and Derek's grip on me loosened.

I threw him to the side, where he crashed through a small wooden end table, splintered pieces surrounding him on the ground.

Derek shook his head at me, but when he rose, he headed for Ryan, shouting, "Let's end this!"

I grabbed one of the larger broken pieces of the end table and shot toward Derek. I connected with Derek at the same time he connected with Ryan.

A jab to the jaw and Ryan slumped to the floor.

Derek didn't go in for the kill, however. He turned to me, eyes widened in shock, the tip of the makeshift wooden stake pointing through his chest at me, accusing. "You…killed…me," he uttered.

Derek disintegrated. I watched his body slowly turn to ash that fell to the carpet before blinking entirely out of existence. Like he had never existed at all.

Ryan moaned while he slowly regained consciousness. We sat on the carpet, me cradling his head in my arms, wishing I could cry. Like a human. Conflicting thoughts zigzagged back and forth in my mind, fighting with each other for dominance.

I killed my sire.

He tried to kill Ryan.

I killed my sire.

He killed many humans.

I killed my sire.

Ryan's eyes opened, stilling the circular thoughts in my head. His strong heartbeat assured me he would be okay. Derek's punch might have knocked him unconscious, but nothing appeared broken. Ryan smiled briefly before frowning. Remembering. He struggled to sit up. To get away from me. We both scrambled to our feet. Ryan's gaze moved wildly around the room, looking for Derek.

"He's gone," I explained.

"You let him leave," he responded incredulously.

"No." I hesitated.

"Then where is he?"

I winced at his anger. "He's gone. Really gone."

Ryan shook his head, not understanding.

"I…staked him."

Ryan snorted. "Please, tell me the truth."

The hurt I saw before returned to his eyes. I sighed. "It is the truth." I sat on the plush couch, running my hands over the soft ridges of the corduroy.

"Still with the vampire nonsense."

"It's not nonsense." I made eye contact, begging him to believe me. I didn't want to have to provide him with a visual. But, I would.

He broke eye contact first. "If you aren't going to tell me the truth, I think you should leave."

I stood and approached him. His heartbeat increased. "Look at me," I commanded. He struggled but ultimately obeyed, his eyes wild. I didn't like using this ability. Except I needed him to understand. My fangs descended and I bared them at Ryan, who blanched.

"Ohmigod," he whispered. "That can't be."

"It is," I assured him.

"Vampires don't exist."

"Yes, we do."

"No, you don't."

"Yes, we do," I repeated. I couldn't help but smile at the childlike turn of the conversation. I reached out and he flinched away. My smile dropped. I returned to sitting on the couch. To my surprise, he moved to sit beside me on the couch.

"Yes, you do," he said in wonder.

"Yes, we do." I put my hand on his knee and this time he didn't move away.

"Where is Derek?" he asked again.

"He's gone. I staked him. I killed him." This last statement escaped my mouth before I could stop myself. I felt Ryan's eyes on me in response. I turned my head to meet his gaze.

"It's like the movies? Poof?"

I smiled sadly and nodded. "Yeah. Poof."

"He was a bad person…vampire. Murderer." His eyes clouded. "Are you?"

"A vampire? Yes," I said, wondering about a concussion.

"A murderer," he clarified.

"No," I answered emphatically. My eyes widened. "Yes. Today."

"That was self-defense," Ryan argued.

I tilted my head, considering. "Yes."

"How do you live?"

I knew what he was asking. "Bottle service," I explained with a wry smile.

He arched an eyebrow. "Have you always…survived…like that?"

"No, in the past, we had acolytes."

"Acolytes?"

"Humans who willingly provided what we needed." I winced at the sudden increase in his heartbeat. "They never died by my hand. Or anyone I knew," I hastened to add.

Ryan nodded. "You feel bad about killing Derek?"

I nodded.

"Why?"

"He wasn't just my husband. He was my sire."

Ryan's eyes reflected confusion.

"He made me. He turned me."

Ryan heard the anger in my voice. "You didn't want him to?"

And there it was. My opening to finally tell him my story. "You accused me of trying to prove Jim guilty because I knew Derek was guilty and I was protecting him." Ryan opened his mouth and I put up a hand to stop him. "Please, let me get this out." He nodded.

"You were partly right. I did want to prove Jim was guilty. And it was because of Derek." Ryan's expression hardened. "Not in the way you think." I took a deep breath, saw Ryan's quizzical expression, and laughed.

"No, I don't have to breathe. After 29 years as a human and 92 as a vampire trying to blend in with humans, it's habit. And, yes, I'm 121 years old." Ryan looked stunned, so I just continued.

"I wanted to prove Jim guilty because I have…trust issues," I started with a shrug. "In my experience, people are not trust-worthy, so when someone appears to have done something bad, well, usually they have."

Ryan interrupted. "Hey, I'm divorced because of a cheating spouse. I understand trust issues."

I managed a small smile. "True." I looked away, gathering my thoughts. I had never told anyone this story. Other vampires knew, of course, but not from me. And no human had ever been told. "It's more than that.

"Derek and I were in love and to be married. In the weeks leading up to the wedding, he did not appear well. He began to look tired, coughing more and more. Dying, it turned out. The week before our wedding, he coughed into a handkerchief and I saw the blood before he could hide it. He finally admitted to me that he had consumption, what today we would call tuberculosis.

"If you know your history at all, typically once you showed these symptoms, it was a death sentence. We both knew this. Derek insisted we should still get married. Even though I would likely be a widow shortly thereafter, he wanted to make sure I was taken care of, and he was very well-off." I paused; Ryan looked shocked.

"The day of the wedding arrived. On what should have been the happiest day of my life, I was devastated. I knew it was a sham, though I couldn't deny Derek's logic. His parents had died of influenza in 1918, and he had no other family to whom to bequeath the money. Women were still second-class citizens. I knew he was right that his money would help me. And I knew he was suggesting it out of love. Still. I was in such emotional pain that day.

"Given everything, we had decided on a small wedding, at my parents' home. They had no idea how sick he was and I didn't have the heart to tell them. That afternoon, though, when I saw Derek standing near the preacher, he was different. He looked even paler than he had, yet somehow healthier. I couldn't explain it. I walked down the aisle, feeling my trepidation increase with each step and not knowing why.

"When he took my hand, his fingers were very cool. He had been running fevers off and on since the worsening of the symptoms. I didn't know what to make of the change. I wondered if this was some final step. That his death was closer than we had thought."

"We went through the motions of the ceremony. I stumbled through the reception; just a few neighbors we could feign celebrating with. And then it was my wedding night." I looked away from Ryan. "I was a virgin. I didn't know what to expect." I stared at my interlocked fingers moving restlessly in my lap, lost in the memory.

CHAPTER TWENTY-TWO

I lay on the bed, half under the wool comforter. I rub the goose bumps rising where my mildly risqué white nightgown bared my shoulders and décolletage. Derek appears in the doorway, a predatory smile on his lips. Wait. That can't be right. I abruptly sit up, wrap my arms protectively across my chest. I suddenly don't want him to see me and I don't know why. He practically skips to the bed, jumping in next to me. He takes me in his cool arms.

"Don't be alarmed," he whispers in my ear. "Everything is okay now."

I pull away. He doesn't feel right. This doesn't feel right. "What's going on? How do you have so much energy?" All at once I feel hopeful. "Did Dr. Raymond have medicine for you?"

Derek laughs harshly. "Dr. Raymond was useless. Medicine was useless. I found another solution." He looks at me so eagerly, I let my guard down.

"How are you better?"

Fangs descend from his gums.

He cuts off my scream by roughly putting his hand over my mouth. He leans in closer to do so. "Shh, shh, it's okay," he murmurs into my ear, though his hand does not move off of my mouth. I try to push him away, expecting him to be the feeble, sick man he was only a day ago. It's like pushing against a rock. I push harder and he laughs. "Kitten, it's fine. Please stop struggling. I'm better now. Cured." I cease struggling, manage to move my head slightly under his hand so that we are eye to eye again. "Are you going to scream?" I shake my head and he removes his hand. I intake a long, shuddering breath, staring at the still descended fangs. He reaches up to fondle one of them, a gesture almost obscene. I look away and he laughs again.

"You'll get used to them," he assures me.

"I don't understand," I whisper. I don't know what else to say to my husband of five hours.

He unexpectedly leaps out of the bed and spreads his arms wide. "I'm a vampire. I'll never get sick. I'll never die. I'm immortal." He jumps back in bed before I can respond. "I want you to stay with me forever."

Understanding dawns and I gasp. "You want me to be a vampire too?"

Hurt flits across his face. "Don't you want to be with me?"

I hesitate. I married him because I loved him. Maybe this wouldn't be so bad? "What is it like being a vampire?" I ask, tentatively reaching out to run my fingers over his pale, cool skin, and the oh-so-sharp fangs. His smile widens.

"It's wonderful. I have amazing hearing. I can smell everything. I'm incredibly strong." He wraps his arms around me and lifts me clear off the bed for a moment before setting me back down. That one moment is exhilarating – and I wonder. He must see that look in my eyes, because he leans in, earnest now. "We can be together forever."

"But…you can't go outside during the daylight, right? And nobody can know? And, don't you have to eat humans to survive?" I rapid fire ask these questions and he laughs again, gently chucking me under my chin.

"Oh, kitten, it's not quite like that. No, we mostly can't go outside during the day. And, no, your family can't know. But, vampires have evolved. We have human feeders. They don't die," he hurries to assure me, after seeing my horrified expression.

Part of me yearns to be with my love. And there's something enticing about living forever, I recognize. Never getting sick. Never dying.

But. Never basking in the sun. Watching my family and friends die and never know the truth. Derek's gaze hardens as he reads my doubts in my expression.

He smiles seductively, though the word predator flashes in my mind again. "Lay with me first and then make your decision," he suggests.

I am uncertain. But he's my husband; maybe this will make more sense. After. I nod. He leans down to whisper in my ear.

"There's one thing I need to finish," he says, so low I almost don't hear him. His fangs descend and bite into the tender flesh of

my neck. I feel a pinch. As he drinks my lifeforce, I lay unmoving on the bed, my eyes closing. I watch now from above the bed. Waiting.

He notices my eyes remain closed. He shakes me gently and I still don't move. I realize without emotion, from above the bed, that I am likely dying. He's too new at this, doesn't know how to take without killing. He has killed me on my wedding night. I realize this, yet it does not bother me. The scene becomes fuzzy, so I am only vaguely aware of him shaking me harder, calling my name. A slight smile forms on his lips. He tears his own wrist and holds it to my mouth.

The blood drips down my chin onto my pale skin, but enough enters my mouth. I taste the copper flavor and feel the warmth. My own blood reviving me? I begin to suckle, like a child with her mother, and when the scene regains its focus, I realize that's not entirely inaccurate. He killed me; and now I am reborn.

I stopped talking and looked at Ryan. His eyes glistened with unshed tears. He took my hands in his. "He turned you. Against your will," he said the unsayable.

I leapt to my feet and strode away from him, to the wall against which I earlier had collided with my now-dead sire. I placed my hands on the plaster, replaying that scene in my mind, trying to chase away the long ago one.

Ryan walked behind me. "It wasn't your fault. You didn't do anything wrong. You didn't choose this."

I spun around, eyes glittering in rage. He withdrew in surprise. "You think I don't know that? Of course, I know that! I've been living this undead life for nearly one hundred years."

"I'm sorry. I don't know the right thing to say."

My anger extinguished with his words and I sighed. "They don't make Hallmark cards for this sort of thing."

He gave me a half-smile in return. "Why do you feel guilty for killing him?" he asked, the smile faltering.

"Vampires don't kill their sires," I answered simply. "It doesn't matter how or why you were turned. It isn't done."

"What happens next then?"

"I don't know. I'll go to the Family and explain the entire situation." I shrugged. "On the bright side, there's no reason to call the police again. After I explain to the Family what happened, they'll likely pull their strings to get Jim released."

"On the bright side," Ryan echoed. "Thank you for that."

"I haven't done anything yet," I warned.

"But you think they'll take care of it." He sounded so hopeful and trusting.

I smiled. "Yeah, I think they will."

We stared at each other for a moment and I sensed a change in the room. Ryan broke eye contact and I knew what he was going to say before he even opened his mouth. I let him say it anyway.

"Thank you for telling me your story," he began.

I waited.

"It's all too much," he admitted. "I will forever be grateful if you can get Jim released. But…" He trailed off.

"Maybe it wouldn't have happened if my crazy ex-husband hadn't come to Vegas? And maybe my being a vampire is too much for you to accept?"

"Something like that," he conceded. Sadness, desire, and understanding played out across his face.

"It's okay," I told him. I turned to leave. "I understand. Be well."

"You too."

He remained silent, didn't call out to me when I opened his front door, walked through, and closed it. I heard his heartbeat and breathing from inside the house, could tell he was hurting.

Back to the real world. I started my car and drove away from him and everything we'd been through.

CHAPTER TWENTY-THREE

At the stoplight for South Casino Boulevard, I risked the wrath of law enforcement and grabbed my cellphone from the side pocket of my car door.

Code Black

No response arrived following my text. I continued driving to my condo and within minutes I was parked and heading up in the elevator.

A man and a woman stood at attention outside my door when I arrived. They had no heartbeats and were not even pretending to breathe. Maybe it was not a myth that we could turn into bats and fly, I kind of wanted to say to them. Instead, I merely nodded as I approached.

No words were spoken while they followed behind me into the condo. I headed for my dining room table. "Thank you," I offered over my shoulder when one of them closed my front door.

"Tell us what happened," the female vampire commanded once we were seated around my table.

"No preamble?" I joked. It was clear they would not provide their names. I ran my fingers over the wood table, wondering at my nervousness. Why? I didn't do anything wrong. I called them after all. I focused on the woman before me. Surprisingly appeared middle age – we usually got turned younger – with her black hair pulled into a severe bun. Her mouth was pressed into a thin line. Fit the image of a Fixer, I imagined. She did not respond and I told her what happened, starting from the very beginning.

The male vampire lifted a single eyebrow when I shared the part of the story where I staked Derek, but that was the only response or reaction I'd received so far. He vaguely looked like a skinhead, unfortunately, with his bald head and tattoos. The sharp blue suit took the edge off the look.

I gazed down at his reaction, so minimal it spoke volumes, but didn't hesitate in continuing the narrative. When I finished with walking out of Ryan's house, the male and female shared an indecipherable look.

"We'll handle it," the female stated with finality and rose from her seat. The male and I quickly followed suit.

"Ryan will be okay, right?" I hesitated to ask this since the Family made the decision, but I'd finally put my finger on why I was nervous.

"You aren't going to clean him, are you?" There. I put it out there for all to see.

The two exchanged another glance. "We're Fixers, not Cleaners," the male answered. "The human will be fine."

The intensity of the relief I felt only mildly surprised me. "Thank you."

"This will be over within 24 hours," the female explained while she walked toward my door.

"That quickly?" I was genuinely shocked by that turnaround.

The male smiled, tipped an imaginary hat, and nodded at me. "That's our job." I smiled in return. We'd reached the door; the female opened it and they exited. I closed the door behind them and leaned against it. Now what did I do?

Before I could even consider the question, I heard a rapid succession of light taps on the door. Catherine's breathing and heartbeat sounded loud, and my smile returned.

I opened the door, caught her hand still raised and about to knock again. She was breathless but smiled.

"I thought they'd never leave."

I laughed and pushed the door open the rest of the way.

"Can I get you anything?" I offered when we passed the kitchen. Part of me wanted to grab a glass of blood, except, much like alcohol with humans, it could be a distraction. Catherine declined my offer of food or drink and we collapsed onto my couch.

"Are you okay?"

"I'm fine," I assured her. She cocked her head in response, so I didn't think she fully believed me.

"What happened?"

Thus, I found myself explaining for the second time in two hours the events of the past night. At least I didn't have to start at the beginning with her.

"Wait," she interrupted when I got to the part where the Fixers beat me to my own home. "How did they get here so quickly? What is Code Black?"

"I'm honestly not sure how they got here so fast," I admitted. "We *can* move faster than humans, but it's not like we can fly or shape shift into bats or anything. I don't think," I added with a laugh. After we finished chuckling, I explained the Family code system.

"Code Black is for non-emergencies that still have an important time element. Like in this case, with Jim in jail for something a vampire did. Code Blue is for any kind of medical issue. Turning someone you hadn't intended to, garlic poisoning, that sort of thing."

"Garlic can poison you?" Catherine asked, clearly fascinated by this glimpse into vampire life and lore.

I shook my head ruefully. "Unfortunately. It smells phenomenal, but if it touches us, or worse, if we ingest it, we become incapacitated pretty quickly. And in large enough amounts, it can be fatal."

That sobered us both, so I moved on. "Code Red is a true emergency. Anything that needs to be handled right then, typically when a vampire is in danger or the Family is in danger of being immediately exposed."

"You sent a Code Black. They were still here before you."

"Must have been in the neighborhood."

Catherine's cellphone trilled an incoming call in time to her laughter at my little joke.

"This late?" I whispered, glancing pointedly at the clock on my wall. She lifted a single shoulder and accepted the call.

"Hello?"

"Catherine, so glad I caught you," a soft voice greeted Catherine, who rolled her eyes.

"Hello, Barbara, what can I do for you this early?"

A short chuckle came across the line. "Don't pretend you were sleeping," she chastised lightly. "I know you're chatting with Evelyn Jones."

Two sets of eyebrows shot up at this statement. I glanced around, briefly wondering if my condo was bugged, before figuring she just as easily could have tracked Catherine here.

Catherine's face was stretched tight and she barely managed to control her anger.

"Why are you tracking my movements?"

"No need to be upset. The last time Robin spoke with Evelyn, the vampire made it clear that she wouldn't speak to my associate – my lackey – anymore. I'm simply honoring her wishes."

Catherine stuck her tongue out at me and mouthed thank you before returning to the call. "Then why are you calling me?"

"The reason I'm calling you both is to congratulate you on solving the murders. As a city councilwoman, I believe it's important to give credit where credit is due."

I snorted and Catherine clapped her hand over her mouth to silence her giggles. I snatched the phone from her hand. "Do you really expect us to believe that's why you're calling, Madam Councilwoman?"

If she caught the sarcasm in my use of her honorarium, she did not let on. "I did have some follow up questions, Evelyn."

Of course she did.

CHAPTER TWENTY-FOUR

"What can I answer for you?"

Catherine chuckled at my saccharine tone and I shrugged. They say you catch more flies with sugar than vinegar.

"Did you ever find out who the original being targeted for the hit by the Family was?"

I cocked my head, curious about the question and her use of the word *being*. I suspected she knew much more than she let on.

"No. Why do you ask?"

"For the safety of the city."

"That's a convenient non-answer."

I swore I heard an almost imperceptible sigh on the councilwoman's end of the call. "Let's just say I'd rather that individual remained breathing."

The call ended.

I chuckled. "She obviously knows who the target was and wanted confirmation. I wonder what this was really all about."

"I have absolutely no idea," Catherine stated, adding, "She's been fixated on me since I arrived in town."

"That's weird. I wonder how that plays into this individual who's been targeted for a hit. You have no idea why the demon is interested in you?"

"I really don't." She sighed. "We can figure it out later. Back to our conversation that was so rudely interrupted. Fixers are different from Cleaners, which is what Derek was?"

"Yep," I answered, feeling a bit like I was conducting Vampires 101 at the local community college. "Cleaners take care of problems by making people and, rarely, other vampires disappear. Fixers do exactly that – fix anything caused by a vampire or human that doesn't need cleaning but puts the Family at risk of exposure."

"I don't understand. Ryan knowing that you exist puts the Family at risk. Why not leave Jim in jail and kill Ryan?" She looked chagrined when I winced at her question. "Don't get me wrong. I'm glad they aren't handling it that way. Still…" she trailed off. "Vampires are portrayed as vicious blood-suckers for a reason. Present company excluded, of course."

"Of course," I agreed with an eye roll. "Believe it or not, we try to find solutions that result in the fewest number of innocent folks negatively impacted, whether human, vampire, or other. It's also the most pragmatic approach. To not draw unwanted attention from humanity."

"Okay, that makes sense, I suppose. I'm thankful to you for your part, so PTA can get back to business."

"What do you mean?"

"Well, with dead bodies and killer vampires running around, everything's been on hold while it got sorted out."

"The movie's going forward? Even without Derek?"

"Yes! A new producer has come on board. And, don't worry, she's keeping all of the casting the same, so you and Ryan are still co-stars." Catherine must have seen something in my expression because she reached out to put her hand on my arm. "How are you and Ryan?"

"There is no me and Ryan," I answered, failing to keep the sadness from my voice.

"Why not?"

I looked at her incredulously. "You heard what happened at his house!"

"Well, sure," she agreed. "But that's only a blip."

I laughed mirthlessly. "I don't think Ryan considers it only a blip."

"What do you want?"

This question stumped me. I liked Ryan's personality. We had oodles of physical attraction. But...

"Evie, I could practically hear your entire internal conversation just now."

I smiled sheepishly at Catherine. "There are so many moving parts to this," I finally stated.

"So what? Give it some time," she instructed. When I didn't respond, she continued. "I ran away when I found out Alex was an incubus. I needed time to process."

I nodded at her statement, something like hope flaring bright in me. What had I gotten myself into? I liked this man. I shook my head to clear the cobwebs and glanced out my floor-to-ceiling windows at the sun noticeable over the horizon.

"Time for you to go to bed," Catherine advised.

"Indeed." We stood and I walked her to the door. I opened it, leaning against it in a deceptively casual posture. She noticed and paused in the doorway.

"Give him time. You might be surprised."

After a quick hug, she continued down the hall to her condo. "Good luck" floated past the door as I closed and locked it.

With a final glance out my windows, I entered my bedroom, pulled the door firmly closed, and fell into bed, fully clothed, exhausted from the day I'd had.

CHAPTER TWENTY-FIVE

I hopped out of bed as the last rays of the sun vanished with its setting. I snagged a bottle of my favorite O+ blood from the refrigerator, warmed it slightly in the microwave, and downed it in one long gulp. I tossed the bottle in the recycling bin and hopped on my couch. I turned the local news on.

As I had hoped, it was the top story. And apparently had been all day. Elizabeth Addison, an entertainment reporter who sometimes also appeared on the regular news, was interviewing a woman with short curly brown hair and brown eyes, rocking an amazing power suit.

Elizabeth held the microphone to the woman's face, her perfectly coifed brown hair not moving when she nodded at the woman's words.

"Jim has maintained his innocence from the beginning. I'm just glad that this came out before a true miscarriage of justice occurred." I recognized the name at the bottom of the screen. Gina Johnson. Jim's lawyer. Her brown eyes narrowed, but she smiled widely, the gap between her front teeth drawing my eye. "The Las Vegas Metro Police Department has apologized to my client, and they expect to release Jim before the end of the evening." Uh huh. That look coupled with that sentence? I smelled a lawsuit.

The screen changed to show a smoldering vehicle, make and model uncertain. A bubbly Asian stood across the street from it. She indicated the wreck behind her. "According to police, the charred remains found in this vehicle belong to the actual killer of Monica Freeman and Sophie Chase. The department spokesperson declined to provide additional information, other than to state that the unnamed deceased individual in the car is without a doubt the murderer."

I clicked the television off with a sigh of relief. Thank goodness. No more dead bodies. No more worry. Jim could get on with his life. Such as it was, I realized, since his vindication wouldn't bring his wife back to life. I frowned and considered what I had just seen. The Fixers kept their word. They definitely stuck with the old adage – stretch the truth as little as possible. Aside from the actual identity of the crispy critter in the car (probably an unidentified body from the morgue, if I had to guess), an innocent man was freed and the guilty party was gone. If

I also had to guess, the police would never correctly identify the body or release additional information, and in the age of the 24-hour news cycle, I was certain a celebrity or politician would do something to draw attention. And life would go on.

A knock on the door startled me out of my reverie. My jaw dropped when I saw Ryan on the other side through the peephole. Tuning into him, I heard the nervousness in his body language, shifting from foot to foot.

"Hi," I greeted him when I opened the door.

"Hi," he responded.

We stared at each other. My eyes couldn't help but roam over the lithe muscles straining under the black t-shirt molded to his torso. His eyes sparked in response.

"Can I come in?"

"You want to come in?"

Scintillating conversation aside, his presence at my condo floored me. I moved to the side of my doorway so that he could enter.

"Can I get you anything?" I asked out of habit and he chuckled.

"I'm okay, thanks."

Yes, you are, I thought to myself as I watched him walk toward the couch. The man filled out a pair of jeans like nobody's business. I inwardly rolled my eyes and smacked myself. Stop it.

We sat on the couch, mere inches apart. It could have been miles. I bit my lower lip. His eyes zeroed in on the movement and became pools of desire.

Geez, I sounded like a romance novel. But, really, they did.

I cleared my throat. "How's it going?"

Ryan belly laughed. "Sorry. I'm not laughing at you."

"You're not?"

His face fell. "I'm not."

"I'm kidding," I assured him.

"I know. It's not that." He stared out the window. "I love that you have a view of the Fremont area on one side and the Strip on the other."

I cocked my head at the non-sequitur.

He looked directly at me. "Thank you."

I heard the sincerity in his voice, but there was an undercurrent of something else. "I let the Family know and they took care of it." I shrugged. "We always fix our messes."

Ryan looked abashed unexpectedly. "Still."

"You're welcome," I responded simply.

"I didn't know if you'd see me," he said quietly.

My lack of response created an awkward moment. The seconds stretched by.

"Say something. Please."

"I don't know what to say. I didn't think I'd see you again." Though I certainly had hoped, I didn't add aloud.

"I didn't think I'd see you again, either. But I wanted to say thank you."

"Okay."

"I hurt you."

"Yes."

"I was so focused on Jim that –" He shook his head. "That's no excuse. I messed up. I'm sorry."

"I forgive you."

We stared at each other. My arms ached to hold him. My lips—

Ryan pulled me into his arms and our lips met. Soft at first, giving way to deeper desire. We melted into each other, the blood coursing through his veins warming me through my clothing. I clutched him closer and he moaned in response. Our lips separated but we stayed in each other's arms. I rested my head on his shoulder, allowing his heartbeat to surround me. This felt so right.

"I guess that answers that," he murmured into my hair. I felt the rumble through his chest when he spoke.

"Answers what?"

"How you feel about me?"

I nestled in even closer. "I didn't think that was ever in doubt." He tensed and I pulled away.

Not touching now, we gazed at each other, such conflicting emotions. "When I heard Jim was going to be released tonight, the first person I wanted to call was you." He half-smiled. "I picked up the phone so many times, even scrolled to your number. I never pushed Call. I tried texting. I never pushed Send."

"Yet, you're here now?" I was almost afraid to ask, to shatter the moment that was building.

"I waited for the sun to start going down since I figured you would be sleeping." He grinned in response to my giggle. "Then I grabbed a Lyft over. I wanted to see. To see you. To see if…"

"I'm glad you did. But."

The light in his eyes dimmed. "But what?"

"I don't know if this is the right thing to do," I admitted helplessly.

Needing to move, I stood and walked to the sliding glass door. I opened it a hair to feel the wind on my face. Ryan moved behind me, snaked his arms around my waist, and rested his head against mine.

"We can work on our trust issues together."

I rotated in his arms so that we were pressed together. His reaction mirrored my own. I kissed him lightly on the lips.

"Yes, we can," I agreed and he smiled. "That doesn't solve the bigger problem."

"That you're a vampire," he said flatly.

"Yes. I'm an undead immortal being. And you're a living mortal."

I closed my eyes against even the thought. "I don't know how we can do it. Me watching you grow old and dying. You becoming bitter when I stay forever young and beautiful."

He smiled at my attempted humor.

"Why do we have to decide my entire life and your entire afterlife right now?"

"Live more in the moment?"

"Yeah."

"Vampires don't really do that well. We're usually in it for the long game; since we have all the time in the world. Typically," I added, as an image of Derek with the stake in his chest flashed in my mind.

"Don't think about that," Ryan responded, and I almost wondered if he heard my thought.

"So, you're suggesting we don't focus on the happily-ever-after?"

"Nope. How about, happily-for-a-human-lifespan," he offered.

I laughed. "Ugh, no. I like your other idea better. Living in the moment. Happily-one-day-at-a-time."

"Happily-one-day-at-a-time," he agreed. "And if one day, we decide to have that bigger talk, we will," he promised.

"We will," I echoed.

Our lips met in a replay of our tender kiss from before. I relished the feel of his lips on mine, his arms holding me against him, our legs intertwined. We separated and he smirked.

"Besides, Catherine told me the movie's a go again with a new producer. You'll see me every night for three weeks anyway."

"I guess I'll see you on set!"

"I'm so glad you could meet me for drinks," the green-haired, green-eyed being sitting across from me said with a wide smile.

We were at a paranormal café, *Soprannaturale*, Italian for supernatural. The owner was a werepanther from Italy. Tucked behind some nondescript storefronts on Main Street, it was unlikely an unsuspecting human would stumble upon it.

"Thank you for inviting me, Ms. Fynn," I responded with my own smile.

"Please call me Mia."

"Thank you, Mia."

"I wanted to meet with the leads of *Vampire Nights* before filming recommences, since I'm coming in late."

"You're a step up from our last producer," I quipped, though felt a stab of pain at the thought of

Derek. I didn't regret killing him exactly, but still. He had been my husband and sire.

Mia must have seen something on my face because she reached over to take my hand in hers. "I know I'm not a vampire, but as a fellow being different from most, I can sympathize with what you're going through."

"Thank you for that," I told her sincerely. "I'm looking forward to no more unexpected deaths and smooth sailing for the entertainment industry in Las Vegas and for Catherine's company, the Paranormal Talent Agency. That's not too much to ask, right?"

THANK YOU!

Thank you so much for supporting my work and reading this book. I truly hope you enjoyed reading it as much as I did writing it.

If you liked the book, please consider leaving a review online.

Just a few lines would be great. Reviews are not only the highest compliment you can pay to an author, they also help other readers discover and make more informed choices about purchasing books in a crowded online space. Thank you so much in advance.

If you didn't like the book or have concerns, please email me directly at
heather@heathersilvio.com

ABOUT THE AUTHOR

Heather has written fiction and nonfiction; she is also an actress and licensed psychologist. When she isn't working, she channels her inner flapper as a 1920s jazz and blues singer.

Visit http://www.heathersilvio.com for more information and to sign up for her New Releases and Appearances Newsletter.

9 781732 693807